A few minutes later, Mark reached the branches just below the platform. He grabbed another branch and planted his foot on a smaller one. He was just about to pull himself up on to the platform when there was a loud *crack!* and the branch supporting his foot snapped.

For one terrifying second, Mark was certain he was going to die. In a desperate attempt to save himself, he threw his hands up to grab for anything. Suddenly he felt two hands go around his wrists.

He stared up and found Henry above him, his arms extended down over the edge of the platform, holding him.

He was the only thing between Mark and certain death. Mark's heart was beating so fast he could feel it all over his body. Adrenalin and fear raced through him. He stared up into Henry's face, but the smile he was used to seeing was gone. Henry gazed back at him with an empty, almost disinterested look.

Mark grunted and kicked his feet, trying to find a branch. Looking down for a foothold, he saw for the first time how sickeningly high in the air he hung. In a flash his head snapped back up as he stared pleadingly into Henry's eyes.

Henry's lips began to move. "If I let you go, do you think you could fly?"

Todd Strasser

The Good Son

Based on the screenplay by Ian McEwan

FANTAIL

To Andrew, a dedicated reader

FANTAIL BOOKS

Published by the Penguin Group
Penguin Books Ltd, 27 Wrights Lane, London W8 5TZ, England
Penguin Books USA Inc., 375 Hudson Street, New York, New York 10014, USA
Penguin Books Australia Ltd, Ringwood, Victoria, Australia
Penguin Books Canada Ltd, 10 Alcorn Avenue, Toronto, Ontario, Canada M4V 3B2
Penguin Books (NZ) Ltd, 182–190 Wairau Road, Auckland 10, New Zealand

Penguin Books Ltd, Registered Offices: Harmondsworth, Middlesex, England

First published in the United States by Pocket Books, a division of Simon & Schuster Inc. 1993
First published in Great Britain by Fantail 1993
1 3 5 7 9 10 8 6 4 2

Fantail Film and TV Tie-in edition first published 1993

Printed in England by Clays Ltd, St Ives plc

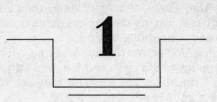

FOR AN INSTANT, TWO CIRCLES HUNG SIDE BY SIDE IN THE
light blue Arizona sky. One was the yellow sun, the
other a black-and-white soccer ball. Mark Evans, age
twelve, caught his breath and positioned himself
under the one that was falling. It struck his chest with
a dull thud and bounced onto the green grass before
him.

"Go! Go! Go!" "Defense! Defense!" "Score!" The
shouts and cheers were coming from everywhere.
They came from the sidelines, where more than a
hundred parents, teachers, and students watched,
some standing stock-still, others jumping up and
down enthusiastically. They came from Mark's teammates, who now spread out beside him as he began to
dribble the ball down the field. And they came from
the opposing players, yelling at each other to get into
position.

Although he was somewhat small for his age, Mark
was an able soccer player, and dribbling the ball was
second nature to him. His eyes scanned the field
ahead, looking for a teammate to pass to or a foe to
fake around. Two kids from the opposite team were

closing in on him, and Mark deftly passed the ball to his left. Alan Parks, the right wing, trapped it and passed it back, leaving the hapless defensemen out of position and scrambling behind.

As he dribbled across the midfield line, Mark could see teammates to his right and left, and two nervous fullbacks from the other team backing up. He knew he'd have a good clean shot at a goal.

He could almost see the ball flying past the goalie and getting caught in the netting. . . .

Breeet! The ref's whistle blew, halting the game. Mark stopped, puzzled, and ran his fingers through his straight brown hair. He was certain his team wasn't offside and he hadn't seen anyone commit a foul. Mark instinctively looked to the sidelines. There he saw something that made him freeze: his father, holding Mark's red and blue warmup jacket. Coach Robbins was waving for him to come off the field. Jason Wicks was coming in to substitute for him.

Mark knew the reason he'd been taken out of the game had nothing to do with sports.

It was his mother.

For a few brief moments back in the game he'd managed not to think about her. But now the thought sent a cold shiver through him. He started to jog slowly off the field. As Jason ran by, he patted Mark sympathetically on the shoulder.

Everyone knew about his mother.

Mark reached the sidelines. He was only half aware of Coach Robbins telling him he'd played a good game. Meanwhile, his father stepped toward him, holding the warmup jacket open for Mark to slip on.

"It's not . . ." Mark couldn't finish the sentence. It couldn't be the end. Not yet.

"No." Jack Evans shook his head. Jack was a handsome man of average height in his early forties.

He was wearing a gray suit that was slightly wrinkled around the knees and elbows.

"Then why?" Mark asked.

"Dr. Porter thinks it might be soon," Jack said. "He said you should come now."

They started back toward the parking lot. The winter Arizona air was dry and the temperature was in the upper seventies. A roar went up from the crowd behind them, but Mark didn't turn around.

"You aren't gonna call the relatives and tell them to come, are you?" Mark asked.

His father was quiet for a moment. Then he said, "Yes, Mark, I am," in a halting voice.

So this was it.

Mark felt a pang deep within. His father had once told him that he wouldn't call the relatives until the end was truly upon them. Ever since then, it had been the one question Mark always asked. As long as the relatives hadn't been called, there was hope.

The hospital was the color of red sandstone and surrounded by gravel gardens and assorted cactus. As Mark and Jack walked down the long corridor, the late-afternoon sun sent orange shafts of light through the open windows and doorways. It was winter, and the sun, as always, seemed to be in a hurry to turn red and disappear behind the mountains in the west.

The hall smelled of medicine. Mark's heart beat fast and he experienced the mixture of dread and longing he always felt when he came to the hospital. Ahead was his mother's private room, and as he and his father approached, Dr. Porter, wearing his white medical jacket and stethoscope, stepped out of the room. The balding older man looked over his bifocals at Mark and Jack. Sometimes in the past he'd smiled when he saw them coming. Today he did not.

Dr. Porter met them outside the door.

"Can we go in?" Jack asked.

"She's asleep," Dr. Porter said. He glanced quickly at Mark. "But I think this might be a good time for Mark to see her."

"Thanks, Doctor," Jack said. He and Mark started toward the doorway, but Dr. Porter touched Jack's arm.

"Jack, could you stay out here for a moment? There are a few things I think we should speak about."

Without his father, Mark hesitated by the door. But Jack Evans nodded slightly, to say that he should go ahead.

Mark stepped into the dimly lit room. The lights were off and the shade had been pulled down, allowing only a thin shaft of reddish sunlight in. Janice Evans lay propped up by pillows, her sunken, ringed eyes closed and her mouth slightly agape. Thin green tubes ran from a tank of oxygen into her nostrils, and a rack with several plastic bags of IV solution hung over the bed and fed down through a long tube into the back of her hand.

Mark felt a lurching sensation. His mother had literally wasted away from a beautiful robust woman into a gaunt, hollow-cheeked, gray-skinned wraith. Even though Mark had seen her several times in this state, it still seemed impossible to him that this was really happening.

That his mother was really dying.

He quietly sat down in a chair beside the bed. Out of a sense of curiosity and impossible hope, he glanced around at the equipment and at the things on her night table, as if there might be something there that would indicate her condition was actually improving, despite the grim look on Dr. Porter's face.

But nothing was different. All the equipment necessary to keep his mother alive was still there. The vase

4

of roses was still on the night table, only the roses had started to wilt. Next to them was a photograph in a silver frame. It was a photograph of his mother in a long white dress, a big smile on her face, walking with Mark through a peach grove with the peach trees in bloom. It seemed impossible that the photo had been taken only the spring before.

Mark reached into the pocket of his warmup jacket and took out the wooden elephant he'd made for her in shop class. It wasn't the greatest thing he'd ever made, just the outline of an elephant cut out of a flat piece of wood. But he knew his mother liked animal carvings and he wanted her to have it. He got up and reached across her to put it on her night table. By accident, he bumped the vase with the wilted roses and had to grab it quickly to keep it from falling over.

Janice Evans's eyes flickered and opened. For a moment Mark and she just stared at each other, and Mark had the feeling she didn't know where she was. Then she seemed to focus on him, and a small smile appeared on her cracked, chapped lips.

"Mark, darling . . ." She spoke slowly and with effort, but even in her debilitated state Mark could feel the aura of love that seemed to emanate from her.

"Hi, Mom." Mark slid back into the chair.

"Why didn't you wake me?" his mother asked.

"I thought you probably needed the sleep."

"You know I'd rather see you," Janice said. "I've been waiting for you. To talk to you."

Mark stopped breathing for a moment. He had been dreading this. Did she want to say goodbye? Or tell him how he had to be strong? Or talk about all the things he'd have to do after she was gone? Mark couldn't bear it. He quickly tried to distract her by pointing to the carved elephant on the night table.

"Look what I made for you," he said.

Janice turned her head slowly, and Mark regretted

not getting the carving himself and holding it up where she could see it.

"It's beautiful, honey," Janice whispered. "Thank you."

"I made it in shop class," Mark said. "Actually, I sort of got in trouble. See, we were supposed to be making lamps, but I really wanted to make this. Anyway, Mr. Roberts . . ."

Mark's words trailed off. He'd wanted to keep talking, to tell any old stupid story that would prevent his mother from saying what she wanted to say. But his mother slipped her hand over his, and in her eyes he could see that she knew he was just trying to stall.

"Has Dad told you everything?" his mother asked.

Mark stared at the floor, trying to fight off the tears that felt as if they were about to spurt unwanted into his eyes.

"Yes, Mom," he whispered.

"Then you know there's going to be some difficult times ahead," his mother said. "You're going to have to be strong."

Mark shook his head. He couldn't stand hearing her talk about what it would be like when she was gone.

"Mom . . ." he started to say.

"Don't worry, Mark," his mother said softly. "I'll always be with you. Always."

Mark looked up at her curiously. The effort to speak had made her tired. Mark could feel her grip on his hand weakening. He placed his other hand on hers and held it.

"I know, Mom," he whispered. "You're not going to die. I promise. You're not going to die, because I won't let you."

He could tell his mother was fading. The effort to talk had caught up to her. But for one brief moment she looked back into his eyes, and he could have sworn she was agreeing with him. Her lips moved slightly, and it seemed she was repeating that word again.

Always . . .

She wasn't going to die. Not really.

He wouldn't let it happen. He *couldn't* let it happen. . . .

Then her eyes closed.

A sense of panic grabbed Mark.

But then he saw her chest rise and fall slightly, and he relaxed. She was still breathing.

Mark heard footsteps behind him and then the scrape of chair legs. His father pulled a chair up beside him. Jack stared at his wife for a moment and then turned to Mark.

"Has she been sleeping?" he asked.

"She was awake for a few seconds," Mark said.

"Did she say anything?"

Mark nodded. Jack waited for his son to say more, but when Mark didn't, he didn't push it. Each of them had to find his own way of coping with what was about to come.

2

HE HAD NO CLEAN SOCKS. MARK SQUATTED DOWN AND peeked into his dresser drawer, hoping there might be one last clean pair stuck in a rear corner. But there weren't any. He straightened up and scanned his room. The wicker hamper in the corner was overflowing with dirty clothes. His desk was covered with papers, magazines, and computer disks. The shade on his window hung crookedly and his bed was unmade.

It hadn't always been this way.

He went downstairs to the kitchen. The dishes from the previous night were still in the sink. A hanging philodendron in the kitchen window appeared to be shriveling from lack of water. Mark watered it and looked around. The kitchen looked dingy. It had never looked like that before.

He pulled open the refrigerator. Immediately a sour odor wafted into his nose. The milk. Holding his nose, he took the milk container out and went over to the sink. He ran the water and then emptied the container. The milk came out in lumps.

"We've got enough in the bank and accounts due to carry the payroll another three weeks." His father came in, talking on the portable phone. "Well, I don't know what we'll do after that. Yes, I know Japan's ready to sign, but I can't go there now. No, you're right, Jim can't do it. It has to be me. Look, either they'll wait or they won't. Sure, sure. Hey, you happen to know a good bankruptcy lawyer? Sure, talk to you later."

His father hung up and rubbed his face with his hands. He had dark rings under his eyes. Mark sometimes woke up in the middle of the night and heard him banging around, unable to sleep.

"Sleep okay?" his father asked.

Mark nodded. "How about you?"

Jack Evans smirked. "All things considered, I'm lucky I got any sleep at all."

"Is something wrong at work?" Mark asked.

"What's wrong at work is that I'm not there."

Mark frowned. "But you go every day."

"You're right," his father said. "I'm sorry. That's not what I meant. I go there, but I'm not there. Know what I mean?"

"Yeah," Mark replied. "I'm like that at school. Only the school doesn't need a bankruptcy lawyer."

Jack Evans smiled at his son. "Neither do I . . . yet." He pulled open the refrigerator and wrinkled his nose. "Uh-oh."

"It was the milk," Mark said. "Don't worry, I already got it."

His father stared into the refrigerator. "Not much to eat, is there?"

"If you give me some money, maybe I could stop on the way home from school and buy some stuff," Mark said.

"I appreciate the offer," Jack said, closing the refrigerator door. "Tell you what: Grab your books and we'll hit the drive-through at Micky Ds."

"Deal," Mark replied. He ran up to his room,

grabbed his schoolbooks, and headed back downstairs, where his father waited with his briefcase. Jack opened the front door, and Mark was just about to go out when they heard the phone ring behind him.

Mark stared at his father. Every time the phone rang it sent a chill through him.

"Wait here," Jack said, and he went back into the kitchen.

Mark let the door close and listened, but his father hardly said anything. Just a few "uh-huhs" and an "I understand." Mark heard the receiver click back down on the hook. Suddenly the house was very quiet. Mark felt a chill and a sense of dread.

It can't happen, he thought. *I promised her I wouldn't let it happen. . . .*

"Mark?" he heard his father say.

"Yes, Dad?"

"You'd better come in here for a moment."

The relatives flew in. His mother's mother came from Florida and a sister came from Oregon. Some cousins came from Texas, and his father's brother Wallace came from Maine. Somebody called a cleaning service to make the house look nice. Everyone told Mark how sorry they were and what a great person his mother was and how they wanted Mark to come visit them during summer vacation.

The funeral was held in the Spanish-style Methodist church Mark attended two or three times a year. Then they all got into limousines and went out to the cemetery, a patch of green grass, monuments, and headstones in the middle of the desert.

It was late morning, and the winter sun burned down on their heads. Mark felt hot in his blue blazer and gray slacks. The palm fronds in the trees around them rustled in the light breeze, and a single hawk soared on a thermal high above. Out beyond the cemetery walls, some sagebrush rolled slowly along the reddish-brown earth past the scrub brush and occasional cactus.

Mark felt his father's hand on his shoulder as he stared at the open hole in the ground and at the shiny, dark wooden casket beside it. A dozen yards away, two men in jeans and T-shirts sat in the shade created by a backhoe and waited. One of them wore a red bandanna around his forehead and smoked a cigarette. It seemed like a pretty ironic thing for someone who worked in a cemetery to do.

A priest wearing a black shortsleeve shirt and a white collar opened a Bible and began to read: "I am the resurrection and the life, sayeth the Lord. He that believeth in me, though he were dead, yet shall he live: and whosoever liveth and believeth in me shall never die. . . ."

Shall never die . . .

Mark repeated the words in his mind.

Shall never, ever die . . .

He looked at the faces of his mother's relatives and friends and was surprised to see that many of them were looking back at him. As if somehow he were the center of attention and not his mother.

He knew it was only because they felt sorry for him.

The kitchen counters and table were covered with platters of food. His mother's friends fussed and cut and poured for the crowd of people who had arrived in a surprisingly festive mood. It was somewhat perplexing for Mark, who had never attended a funeral before, to see that people who had been sobbing by the side of his mother's grave less than an hour before were now talking, if not cheerfully, at least animatedly in his living room.

Even more perplexing, and annoying, were all the people who wanted to kiss him and touch him and rub his head and pat his shoulder and tell him how sorry they all were. He knew they meant well, but so many of them were people he hardly knew; and while he didn't want to be mean, he wished they'd keep their hands to themselves.

Finally, after a dozen people had said how wonderful his mother was, it got to be too much for him. He let himself out the sliding-glass door of the kitchen and into the backyard. He shut the door behind him, and the voices suddenly faded away, replaced by the sound of a jet roaring high above and some kids yelling as they played in the street on the other side of the fence. Mark walked across the grass, which had been green in previous years but was now turning brown with neglect.

New voices reached his ears.

"The opportunity won't wait forever, Jack. For the sake of your company and your employees, you've got to go."

Mark came around the corner of his house and was surprised to find his father and his uncle Wallace standing by an orange tree, talking. As soon as they saw him, the talking stopped.

"Hey, Mark, what are you doing out here?" his father asked solemnly.

"I just had to get outside for a while," Mark said.

"You all right, son?" Wallace asked. He was a few years older than Jack and had short, wavy blond hair that he combed back.

"Yeah, I guess," Mark said. It was obvious that his uncle and father had been talking about something they didn't want him to know about. "Uh, I'll catch you later," he said, and started off in a different direction.

"You sure you're okay?" his father asked.

"Yeah, pretty sure," Mark replied.

Jack Evans watched his son walk away. Then he turned back to his brother. "I can't leave him at a time like this, Wallace. He needs me."

"We're not talking about an eternity, Jack," Wallace replied. "It'll be two weeks."

Jack shook his head. "I just can't do it."

"It's not like you'd be leaving him with strangers. I'm your brother, Jack. We're family."

"I guess that's why we see each other only at funerals," Jack replied. Wallace winced, and Jack immediately regretted his words. Two years earlier Wallace had lost his two-year-old son, Richard. The boy had drowned in the bathtub in Wallace's home in Maine.

"I'm sorry, Wallace," Jack quickly apologized. "I don't know why I said that. I know you're just trying to help."

"It's a bad time," Wallace said. "Believe me, I understand."

"How is Susan?" Jack asked. Susan was Wallace's wife.

"You mean, in terms of what happened?" Wallace asked.

Jack nodded.

Wallace sighed. "She has good days and not such good days. It's something you never stop living with, something you never forget. You wake up in the middle of the night wondering if there was anything you could have done differently. I still don't have an answer."

"God, Wallace," Jack said, shaking his head. "I'm sorry it happened to you. If something like that happened to me, I don't know what I'd do."

"Hey, something like that *has* happened to you." Wallace put his hand on his brother's shoulder. "I've known you your whole life, Jack. You've never had to

13

face anything like this before. Believe me, Jack, this is the time when you have to let other people in. You've got to let us help you."

"I just feel that leaving Mark now would be the worst thing I could possibly do," Jack said. "I mean, he's just lost his mother. Now his father's going to disappear too?"

"He's old enough to understand," Wallace said. "Susan and I will take care of him while you take care of business. You can't put it off any longer, Jack. Your company's on the verge of going under."

"I'm not sure I really care," Jack said.

"You've spent half your life building this company," Wallace said. "Throwing it away now won't make anything better."

Jack stared over the backyard fence, past the other houses in the neighborhood and out at the reddish-brown mountains in the distance. "I just wonder now if it was worth it. I mean, all the weekends I worked. All those trips I took away from the family. Maybe I should have had a regular nine-to-five job and stayed home."

"Jack." Wallace put his hands on his shoulders. "Janice didn't get sick because you worked hard. One has nothing to do with the other. You still care about your future, don't you? You care about Mark's future."

"Of course I do," Jack said.

"Then make sure he has one. You said if you can close this deal in Tokyo, it could turn the company around."

"Maybe," Jack replied. "It's never a sure thing until they've signed on the bottom line."

"But it's your only chance to save the company," Wallace urged him. "You've got to try it."

Jack glanced back at the corner of the house where

Mark had been a few moments before. Could he leave him? Even for two weeks?

"Listen, it'll be good for Mark to be with other kids," Wallace said as if he'd read his brother's mind. "I mean, you saw him a few minutes ago. He's lost around all these adults. If he comes out to my place he'll have Henry and Connie to play with all day."

Jack sighed and gazed out at the mountains again. His brother had made a number of good points. He hated like hell leaving Mark for two weeks, but if he tried to look past those two weeks, everything Wallace said rang true. He glanced back at his brother.

"What does Susan say?"

"You know Susan," Wallace said with a slight smile. "She told me not to come back to Maine without him."

Jack blinked. Something about the idea of Wallace taking Mark home on the airplane didn't feel right. "No," he said. "I'll bring him myself. The Japanese will wait an extra week. Mark and I need some time together."

"Fine," Wallace replied. "I'll tell Susan to expect you and Mark sometime next week."

3

THE LEFTOVERS WERE WRAPPED IN CELLOPHANE IN THE refrigerator. The relatives and friends had gone. It was late. Jack and Mark sat at the kitchen table. A steaming mug of coffee rested before Jack.

"How are you doing, Mark?" his father asked.

"Please don't keep asking me that, Dad," Mark replied. "I'm doing the same as I was before."

"Okay," Jack said with a nod. "Hungry?"

Mark shook his head.

Jack softly blew the steam away from the coffee mug. "Look, there's something I have to talk to you about."

There was something in his father's voice that scared Mark. "What?"

"How'd you like to drive to Maine with me?" Jack asked.

Mark frowned. "Why?"

"Because I have to go to Japan for a couple of weeks. Wallace said he and Susan would like to have you stay with them."

Mark shook his head. "No way."

Jack wasn't surprised. "I didn't think you'd be

interested, but I'm afraid it's something we may have to do."

"I don't want to go," Mark said. "I want to stay here with you . . . and Mom."

The furrows in Jack's forehead wrinkled. It seemed like an odd thing to say, but he knew better than to challenge his son on it. "I have to go to Japan, Mark. If I don't, my company's going to be in big trouble. And if that happens, you and I will be in trouble too."

"Then why can't I come to Japan too?" Mark asked.

"You can't," Jack said. "First of all, it's prohibitively expensive. Second, I'll be in meetings all the time. There'll be nothing for you to do all day."

"I'll take walks," Mark said.

"No, you simply can't come," his father said. "Believe me, it's not that I don't want you to come. You just can't. And if I didn't have to go, I wouldn't. You have to believe me."

Mark shrugged and nodded.

"Now, I guess I could make arrangements for you to stay with one of your friends around here," his father said. "But I think it would be better if you spent some time with your aunt and uncle. I have a feeling we'll be seeing a lot more of them from now on anyway. They've got a son named Henry who's about your age, and a daughter named Connie who's a few years younger. They're your first cousins. You've seen pictures of them."

Mark had seen the pictures. Not that you could tell much from a picture, but at least the kids didn't look like dorks or anything.

"Besides, you've never been to Maine," Jack said. "It will be a good change for you."

Mark stared across the table at his father. Normally he wouldn't say what was on his mind. But this wasn't normal. "I'm just worried I'll be lonely without you."

"Don't worry," Jack said with a slight smile. "After

a week together in the car, you'll be glad to get rid of me."

Mark nodded. It was hard to know at that moment what felt right or wrong, or what he really wanted.

"Oh, one other thing," Jack said. "Make sure you pack the warmest coat you have."

"I don't have a coat," Mark said.

Jack sighed. "Then I guess we'll have to fake it."

The night before they were to leave, Mark's father stayed on the phone in the kitchen for hours, making last-minute arrangements for his trip. Mark watched TV for a while and then went upstairs to his room. He sat on his bed and looked around. His bag was packed and standing by the door. He looked at the Game Boy on his desk and thought about playing it, but then another thought came into his mind.

He was going away.

He had to say goodbye.

He got up and left the room, walking down the hall until he got to the door of his parents' room. It might have been strange, but he hadn't been in that room in months, not since his mom went into the hospital.

He pushed open the door. The lights weren't on, but the room wasn't that dark. The shades were up, and the moon outside was full, filling the room with moonlight. Mark walked slowly around to his mother's side of the bed. Just past it was the vanity table and mirror where she used to sit in the morning and do her hair and put on her makeup. Her brush and blow-dryer were still there, along with some small glass jars of nail polish.

Mark felt a terrible pang in his heart. It was as if she'd never left, he thought. As if she was still there.

Maybe she was.

Maybe he hadn't let her die after all.

The pain in his heart was awful. It just wasn't fair

that his mother was gone. He looked up at himself in the mirror. His eyes glistened with tears that threatened to tumble out and roll down his cheeks. He tried to blink them back.

Maybe she's still here, he told himself. *Maybe she hasn't left.*

But where was she?

A flicker of light in the mirror caught his eye. Mark turned and saw that the closet light was on. He stepped to the closet and opened the door. He was surprised to see that only one thing hung there: his mother's white dress. The one she'd worn that day last spring when they'd walked through the peach grove.

He still remembered it. How alive she was. How happy.

Lit by the flickering light bulb overhead, the dress seemed to glow with a special aura.

Mark wiped the tears from his eyes and stared at it. Could it be?

"Mom?" he whispered urgently. "Are you here?"

There was no answer.

"Just give me a sign," Mark whispered.

He waited, but the dress just hung silently, unmoving, glowing faintly in the light.

4

THE ROAD WAS A RIBBON OF BLACK SNAKING THROUGH the stark desert at midday. The sun was a ball of yellow fire, and through the windshield Jack could see waves of heat ripple off the asphalt that stretched east.

They'd departed only that morning, and already the dashboard was littered with maps, empty cups, and food wrappers. Jack glanced at his son, who was staring down intensely at the gray Game Boy in his hands. Except for an occasional grunt of yes or no to a question about food or bodily functions, Mark hadn't said a word since the trip began. All he'd done was play Game Boy.

They were coming into an area of magnificent buttes and towering peaks.

"Hey, you," Jack said, trying to keep things light. "Fellow passenger. If you ever get tired of level two hundred and sixty-three, you're missing some great stuff out the window."

If Mark heard him, he gave no sign of it. His head remained bowed before the electronic game. The only sound from his side of the car was that ridiculous tinny music that accompanied the Super Mario Brothers.

"Wow!" Jack gasped. "I just saw a coyote with a bazooka chasing a road runner!"

Mark glanced over and worked up a minor smile, just to let his father know that the joke was appreciated. Then he went back to the Game Boy.

Jack knew he wasn't making any progress. Chances were he wasn't going to make any, either, unless he forced the issue. He pulled the car over to the side of the road. The dust on the road shoulder kicked up and drifted past them, and a car shot by, its passengers staring at them curiously.

Jack put the car in park and turned to his son. Even though Mark stayed glued to the Game Boy, Jack could see him tense in anticipation of a confrontation.

"Mark?"

Even now Mark continued to stare at the Game Boy. Moving his thumbs rapidly over the controls, his teeth clamped down on his lower lip.

"I know you're hurting, Mark," Jack said. "But please don't shut me out like this."

Mark ignored him. Despite his best attempts at remaining calm and rational and understanding, Jack could feel himself starting to lose it. Finally he reached over and grabbed the Game Boy away. It took great restraint not to hurl it out the window.

"Now talk to me," Jack said.

"What?" Mark snapped irritably.

Jack steadied himself. It wasn't like Mark to be angry and defiant. Obviously there had to be a lot on his mind.

"Getting angry won't help," Jack said. "Especially since I'm not sure what you're angry about. Is it me? Is it life? Is it Mom? I think about her all the time too."

Mark stared at his father for a long moment. It seemed as if the time had come to tell him.

"I don't know why I have to go to Maine," he said.

"I told you why," Jack said. "I've got to go to Japan. There's no one here to take—"

"She's coming back," Mark interrupted.

"Mark . . ." his father's voice trailed off.

"Maybe she's not gonna come back as herself," Mark said. "But she's gonna come back."

Jack could feel his sense of surprise turn into a sharp, agonizing pain. Maybe he'd overestimated his son's ability to deal with this crisis. Maybe he'd been foolish to think a boy of twelve could assimilate it.

"Listen, Mark," he said softly. "I miss her too. But we have to accept the fact that she's gone."

"No!" Mark shouted.

"Yes."

The next thing he knew, Mark pushed open the car door and started to run.

Jack watched in amazement as his son took off into the desert. He stilled his first impulse, which was to jump out of the car and sprint after him. Instead he got out of the car slowly and made sure the doors were locked.

Mark kept running. He didn't know why and he didn't know where. He just felt like he had to get away.

Away from his father.

Away from what had happened to his mother.

Away from himself.

But then, just as suddenly as he'd started to run, he stopped. Who was he kidding? There was no place to go. He stood for a while with his back to the road. Just as his father had said, there were magnificent bluffs and peaks around him. Not that he cared. Not that he was going to turn around and go back.

Maybe he'd just stand there forever.

No such luck. His father walked up and stood beside him. For a while he just stood there.

Don't say anything, Mark prayed. *Please don't say anything!*

"Well," his father said. "At least you got to look around."

Mark nodded. He felt that if his father said one word about his mother he was going to explode.

"You know, some people shrink inside themselves when they see a desert," Jack said. "It's too big for them. There are no anchor points, nothing to hold on to. Then there are other people like you, Mark. They want to step right out into the middle of it. Your mother was like that. She loved the desert."

Mark turned slowly and looked up at him. He'd never heard that before. "Really?"

"Yeah," Jack said. "I know she didn't come out here much in recent years, but when we were younger, she always wanted to drag me out. Day, night, it didn't matter."

"I never knew that," Mark said, hardly aware that all the anger inside of him had started to melt away.

"You're a lot like her, Mark," Jack said. "Stubborn, strong. Did I ever tell you about the time she talked me into hiking down into the Grand Canyon?"

Mark shook his head. Jack put his hand on his son's shoulder and started to guide him back toward the car.

"Well," Jack said, "it wasn't so much going down that I objected to. It was having to climb back up that I wasn't looking forward to. Of course, that wasn't your mom's style at all. She wouldn't worry about going back up until *after* she got down there."

"Yeah." Mark couldn't help smiling. "That's just like her."

Jack told the rest of the story in great detail. All

23

about going down, and about the long hard trip back up, but how Janice would never admit how hard it was.

Soon they got back to the car. The confrontation was forgotten, and they drove onward toward the approaching night.

5

THEIR JOURNEY TOOK THEM ACROSS ARIZONA AND through Albuquerque, New Mexico, then through the northern part of Texas, where they stopped to have buffalo burgers in a cafe in Amarillo. From there they passed oil wells in western Oklahoma and saw more corn fields in southern Kansas than they ever imagined existed. Missouri was where they stayed in a farmhouse inn that looked as if it was out of *Little House on the Prairie*. They drove through Illinois and visited the first McDonald's ever built, then crossed northern Indiana and cut through the lower eastern corner of Michigan. In Detroit they visited a car museum and then headed into Canada. From there they passed through Toronto and on to Montreal before cutting due east and into Maine.

It was a good trip for both father and son, and by the time they reached the Maine coast, Mark had long since dropped his defenses and allowed some of his boyish enthusiasm to come out.

"Oh, wow!" he gasped the first time the gray-blue Atlantic ocean came into view. They pulled over onto the side of the road. It was a windy, gray day, and they

25

grabbed their jackets out of the backseat. Once they got out of the car, Mark was shivering in no time.

"Oh, man, you didn't tell me it would be *this* cold," he said through chattering teeth as they stood at a guardrail by the side of the road.

"It's not just the cold," Jack said, pulling the collar of his raincoat closed. "It's the wind and the dampness. Maybe we'd better get back into the car."

But Mark shook his head. "I want to see it." He stepped over the guardrail and walked a little way until he'd come to the edge of a low cliff. Below him the waves crashed against huge gray rocks.

"It's big," Mark said, hugging himself and staring out at the ocean covered with whitecaps.

"I know," Jack said. "It's hard to imagine something you can't see the end of."

Mark pointed east. "What if you had a boat and you just kept going and going?"

"You'd hit Europe sooner or later," his father said.

Mark stared down at the rocky shore. "What about a beach?"

"There are a few along the coast, but it's mostly rock like this," his father said. "Not that it matters. From what I remember it's usually too cold to swim in, even in the middle of summer."

"That's a waste," Mark said.

Jack couldn't help smiling. "Well, the ocean is good for a few other things, even if you can't swim in it."

It wasn't long before Mark was too cold to stay outside. They got back in the car and Jack talked about the value of layering clothes to stay warm. Their car followed the winding coastal highway, and soon they came to a white wooden sign welcoming them to Rock Harbor, Maine.

"Is this where Wallace lives?" Mark asked.

"Yup," his father replied as they drove through the center of town. "Pretty place, huh?"

Mark nodded. He'd never seen anything quite like it. All the buildings were either wooden or brick. Some were painted gray or blue, but most were white. The big picture window of the hardware store featured things like snowblowers and electric space heaters. The gas station was having a special sale on snow tires. They passed some really big places that looked like hotels but didn't have signs.

"How come they don't have signs?" Mark asked.

"Huh?" Jack was caught off guard. "What kind of signs?"

"Like the name of the hotel or a vacancy sign," Mark said.

Jack scowled and looked out the window. Then he smiled. "Those aren't hotels, Mark. Those are houses."

"You mean, one family lives in a place like that?" Mark asked in wonder. "They must have really big families around here."

"Well, they used to," Jack said. "I'm not so sure they do anymore."

"Then what do they do with all the extra rooms?" Mark asked.

"Pay a lot to heat them," Jack replied.

It wasn't long before they left town and started on a narrow road along the ocean. Driveways wound down to the road, but it was sometimes impossible to see the houses they led to. Finally Jack turned into a driveway marked "Private."

"Uh, is Uncle Wallace rich?" Mark asked.

"Let's just say he's done well," Jack said with a smile.

"Is he in the same business as you?" Mark asked. "Computer software?"

"No, Wallace ran a mutual fund during the eighties," Jack said.

"What's that?" Mark asked.

"It's sort of like a company that buys shares of stock in other companies and then turns around and sells shares of its own stock to the public," his father explained.

"Why would they do that?" Mark asked.

"Well, it all has to do with picking the right stocks and lowering the risk an investor takes," his father said. "It's a little bit complicated, but basically Wallace did it extremely well."

"So what does he do now?" Mark asked.

"He sort of still does it," his father said. "But at a more relaxed pace."

Mark squinted at his father. "So he is rich."

"Let's just put it this way," his father said. "Wallace's family is comfortable. They don't have expensive things, but they could if they wanted to."

"Okay, gotcha," Mark said.

Their car came to the top of the drive and Uncle Wallace's house came into view. It was a big, rambling white house with a wraparound porch and a view of the ocean. Mark quickly counted four chimneys.

Jack stopped the car and they both got out and stretched.

"Not bad, huh?" Jack asked.

Mark nodded. There was something about the house that felt friendly. Even though it was big, it wasn't formal or foreboding. A couple of bikes stood on the porch, and in the yard was a small backstop for baseball. Mark wasn't sure what he had expected, but he felt relieved.

The front door swung open, and Wallace came out wearing a heavy brown wool sweater, blue jeans, and sneakers. He was slightly bent over, and it took Mark a second to realize he was carrying a young girl on his back. She looked like she was five or six and had blond hair parted in the middle and pulled into pigtails. She must be Connie.

Wallace was smiling and Connie was laughing. Still, Mark felt a little shy and stood back as they came down and greeted his father.

"Hey!" Wallace said, extending his hand. "You made it."

"What a haul," Mark's father said, shaking his hand. "Ten states and Canada in four days."

"Took the northern route, huh?" Wallace said.

"Yeah, I thought it would be more interesting for Mark. He hasn't seen much east of the Mississippi."

Connie began to fidget on Wallace's back.

"Okay, okay," Wallace said with a laugh. "Connie, say hello to your Uncle Jack."

"Hello, Uncle Jack!" Connie shouted.

Wallace winced. "Thanks, hon, that was right in my ear."

"Hi, Connie, how are you?" Mark's father asked.

"Okay." Now Connie got shy and hid behind her father's head.

Jack smiled at his brother. "She's beautiful, Wallace."

"Takes after her mother," Wallace replied. He glanced over at where Mark was standing. "So how's it going, Mark?"

"Pretty good," Mark replied with a timid smile.

"How'd you like the trip?"

"It was okay, except for the flat parts."

"I'm afraid the Midwest doesn't have the exciting terrain you find out west," Wallace said.

"It's pretty nice around here," Mark quickly said.

"Oh, yes," Wallace said. "The ocean and the shoreline. A lot of pretty harbors and islands. I'm hoping we might be able to get up to Acadia National Park while you're here. It's just going to depend on how work goes for the next couple of weeks."

Connie started to squirm on Wallace's back.

"Hey, what . . ." Wallace started to ask but then appeared to remember. "Oh, right. Okay."

He let Connie down, and she came toward Mark and took his hand and started to pull. "Mom said I could show you the house. Come on!"

Mark scowled at Wallace.

"Don't try to resist," Wallace said with a laugh. "She always gets her way."

The kids went toward the house. Jack started to follow, but Wallace reached for his arm to stop him.

"How's he doing?" Wallace asked.

Jack watched as Connie pulled his son up onto the porch. "Okay, I guess. It's hard to tell."

"He doesn't talk about it?" Wallace guessed.

"Not much," Jack said. "We had an incident the first day in the car. Mark keeps insisting that Janice isn't gone. That she's still here. I can't quite get a handle on what he means. Like, does he think she's still physically here? Or spiritually? Or is he talking about her living on in our memories?"

"Think it's something serious?" Wallace asked.

"I don't think so," Jack said. "Probably just what a boy of his age does at a time like this."

Wallace nodded. The two brothers stood quietly in the cold, wet Maine air.

"And how are you doing?" Wallace asked.

Jack shrugged. "I'm best off when I'm feeling numb."

"You guys had a good marriage," Wallace said sadly. "It's times like this that probably make you wish you hadn't."

The mention of marriage reminded Jack of something: "You sure Susan's up to this? I don't want Mark to be a burden."

Wallace forced a smile onto his face. "Believe me,

he won't be. It'll be good for Susan to have a diversion. Come on, let's go in and see her."

Wallace and Jack started toward the house. Ahead they could see that the first thing Connie chose to show Mark was the porch. "See how it goes all the way around the house?" she asked, running around the entire porch to demonstrate.

Mark jogged after her. He was surprised at how stiff his legs felt and how quickly he started puffing for breath, but after four days of doing nothing but sitting in a car, he shouldn't have been surprised. Finally they stopped by the front door.

"Want to see my room first?" Connie asked, filled with childish excitement. "It's upstairs. Eighteen steps."

Connie pushed open the front door, and they stepped into the entryway. Before Connie could pull Mark upstairs, a voice called, "Connie? Are they here?"

An attractive woman with short brown hair and large brown eyes stepped into the hallway that led to the front door. As she walked toward them, her eyes met Mark's and they stared at each other as if in a trance. Mark suddenly had the strangest sensation, as if for that very short span of time there was no one else there except her. He felt goose bumps run down his arms. It felt as if, in some strange way, they immediately shared something. Or maybe it was the feeling that somehow they already knew each other, even though they'd never laid eyes on each other before.

Then Mark heard his father and Wallace come up the front steps behind them and into the house. The spell was broken. Everyone gathered in the entryway together. The woman turned to Mark's father and hugged him.

"Jack," she said, giving him a kiss on the cheek.

"Susan, you look great," Jack said, hugging her back. But Susan was already looking back at Mark.

"You must be Mark," she said.

Wallace gave Mark a playful nudge. "Better run," he said. "I think she's going to hug you."

"Try and stop me," Susan said with a smile.

Mark wasn't sure if Wallace was kidding about running or not. But the next thing he knew, Susan was reaching toward him. She took him in her arms. Mark had the strangest feeling when she did that. He didn't understand what it was, and it could have made him uncomfortable. But as if Susan sensed that, she didn't drag it out.

"I think you're going to like it here," Susan said, stepping back and gazing at him. "We've got the woods and the beach—"

"Beach?" Mark asked, surprised. He glanced back at his father.

"Well, it's not like you can go swimming," Wallace said.

"I don't think it's that," Jack said. "I just prepared him for the rocky coastline. I forgot you had some beach out back."

"Oh, yeah," Wallace said with a smile. "You'll be amazed at what you can find around here."

Now Connie pushed her way into the group and pulled at her mother's sleeve insistently. "Mom, *please,* I have to show Mark the house."

She held out her hand to Mark again, but before he could go with her, Wallace grabbed her.

"Whoa, there," he said with a laugh as he tickled her. "Don't forget, Mark's a member of the family now."

Still holding Connie, Wallace turned to Mark. "If anybody gives you any trouble—especially this little monster—you come to me."

Wallace and Connie started to roughhouse a little. Mark just stood there and watched. He noticed that his father and Susan had backed away from the group and were talking in hushed tones. It wasn't hard to guess that they were talking about his mother.

"How's he taking it?" Susan asked softly.

"Like any twelve-year-old son would," Jack replied. "Pretty hard, I'm afraid."

"Did Wallace tell you about Alice Davenport?" Susan asked.

"No."

"She's a therapist," Susan said.

Jack began to scowl.

"But she's also a friend," Susan hastened to add. "We've known her for years. You'll like her."

"I'm going to meet her?" Jack asked, puzzled.

"We've invited her over for dinner," Susan explained.

It took Jack a moment to sort it all out, but then he realized it had been arranged for Mark.

"You're not mad, are you?" Susan asked.

"No, I don't think so." Jack chose his words carefully. "Let's see how things work out. But even if they don't, I want you to know how much I appreciate everything you're doing."

Susan took his hand and squeezed it. "Janice would have done the same thing."

The atmosphere in the entryway was warm and friendly. Mark watched as Connie roughhoused with her father, and Jack spoke quietly to Susan. He was starting to think that maybe it would be okay here.

"Ahhh!" Connie suddenly screamed and pointed up the stairs. Everyone stopped what they were doing and stared. At the top of the stairs, leering over the banister, a pale, sinister face stared back at them. Mark felt an involuntary shiver. The face reminded

him of advertisements he'd seen for *The Phantom of the Opera.*

For one long stunned moment, no one said a thing. Wallace was the first to speak: "Very funny, Henry. Now come on down."

Henry.

Mark realized it was only a mask. The boy wearing it must be Henry. Taller than Mark, he was wearing a maroon sweatshirt over a denim shirt and jeans. Still wearing the mask, Henry Evans bounded down the stairs and jumped the last five steps, landing with a loud *Thud!* on the entryway floor. Suddenly pretending to have a terrible limp, he staggered toward Mark, making strange, incoherent sounds.

Out of the corner of his eye, Mark saw Susan's look of shock become one of amusement.

"Okay, Henry," Wallace said in a tolerant voice. "Hospitality."

Henry pulled off the mask and smiled as if he were pleased with the effect he'd had on everyone. He was a good-looking, blond-haired boy who seemed quick to smile and filled with energy. Now he handed something to Mark.

Mark looked down and saw that it was another mask.

"I made two," Henry said. "So that we could be brothers."

Mark held the mask to his face and looked at the others. Everyone laughed, but it wasn't because they thought it was funny. It was more like they were just relieved.

Henry put his mask back on too. Now identical, the boys bowed to each other. Susan smiled and ruffled Henry's hair.

"You may not believe this, but this is my darling, beautiful boy," she said with a warm chuckle.

34

6

THE REST OF THE AFTERNOON PASSED QUICKLY. CONNIE insisted on completing the tour of the house with Mark. Mark was certain he'd never been in a house with so many rooms and staircases. They covered three floors, skipping the attic and basement. Then Henry joined them and they walked down to the beach, a patch of dull grayish sand maybe fifty feet long and nestled in a cove of dark forbidding rocks. Rising up on each side of them were tall cliffs. Sea gulls hung in the air above them, and a cold sea mist drifted in from the ocean. For a while they threw stones out into the curling waves, but Mark, who still wasn't used to the wet cold of Maine, started to shiver.

Thankfully, they didn't stay out long. When they got back into the house, they cut through the kitchen, where Susan was starting to prepare dinner.

"Mom, could we have some hot chocolate?" Henry asked.

"Sure, kids." Susan immediately put down the potatoes she'd been peeling in the sink and got out the cocoa. She reminded Mark of his own mother, always ready to drop everything to help someone else. Some of his friends' mothers weren't like that. You'd ask for something and they'd make you wait until they were finished with whatever they were doing before they helped you.

Henry's mother was just taking the milk out of the refrigerator when she noticed that Mark was still shivering.

"Are you cold?" she asked.

"Not now," Mark replied. "I was outside."

Susan frowned. "Well, no wonder. Look at the jacket you're wearing. That may be okay for a cool Arizona evening, but it's not nearly enough for around here."

"It's the heaviest one I have," Mark said with a shrug.

"Then we'll let you use one of Henry's, won't we?" Susan said, glancing at her son.

Mark looked at Henry. For just a second, he could have sworn he saw the coldest look pass over the boy's face. But in an instant it was gone.

"Hey, sure." Henry nudged Mark with a warm, open smile. "We're brothers. What's mine is yours."

Mark smiled back and wondered about the look he'd thought Henry had given him. Did it seem intensely dark and mean?

Maybe he'd just imagined it.

Later, after it started to get dark, they went into the dining room for dinner. They sat at a big table over a rug in the middle of the room. The side of the room that faced the ocean was all windows with white lace shades. On the other side of the room, several large portraits hung on the wall. Two big old-fashioned radiators banged and hissed as they let out steam. At one end of the room, a fire crackled in a stone fireplace.

"Who are those people?" Mark asked, pointing at one of the portraits. He, Connie, and Henry were the only people in the room at the moment. Wallace and Susan were in the kitchen, and Jack was talking to a lady who'd just arrived.

"They're my mom's parents," Connie said.

"No, they're her grandparents," Henry corrected her. Mark had noticed that Henry often corrected his little sister and sometimes seemed very harsh toward her. At other times he seemed very warm and loving. Mark figured this was just the way brothers and sisters were.

"They built this house," Connie explained.

"Actually, they had it built," Henry corrected her again. "It wasn't like they built it themselves with their own hands."

"Okay, everybody," Wallace said as he came in carrying a big tray with a roast on it. "Time to sit."

Mark looked at the table uncertainly.

"We sit down at this end," Henry said. "The grown-ups sit at that end."

Henry sat at the end of the table. Mark sat down catercorner from him, and Connie sat down across from Mark. Now Jack and the woman he'd been talking to entered the room. The woman looked older than Mark's father, but not as old as Mark's grandparents. Mark figured she might be in her fifties. Her hair was mostly gray, and she wore a loose-fitting red dress. She wore gold wire-rim glasses and had a kind smile.

"Mark, this is Alice Davenport," Jack said. "She's a friend of Wallace and Susan's."

"Hi," Mark said with a nod. From the way she and Jack had been talking, Mark sensed that she was more than just a friend of his aunt and uncle's.

"Hello, Mark," Alice said. "Your father's told me a lot about you."

"I hope it was good stuff," Mark replied.

Alice smiled warmly. "Oh, yes, it was."

Mark smiled back. He had a feeling this wouldn't be the last time he saw Alice during his stay in Maine.

"Okay, Henry, you know what to do," Wallace said as he began to slice the roast.

Henry went into the kitchen and returned with a bottle of red wine. Then he went around the table, filling the grown-ups' glasses. Mark watched him. Suddenly Henry caught his eye and winked. Then he lifted the wine bottle to his lips and pretended to drink.

"Daddy, look!" Connie squealed.

Wallace looked up and smiled. "Okay, wise guy, very funny." He handed Henry a plate of food. "Hand this to Mark."

Susan came in from the kitchen and sat down. "Okay, everyone, dig in."

Jack stared down at the thick, rare slab of roast beef on his plate, surrounded by potatoes and broccoli. It was the first good home-cooked meal he'd had in a long time.

"Something wrong?" Susan asked, puzzled.

"No," Jack said with a smile. "It looks . . . good enough to eat."

The adults laughed, although Mark wasn't certain what was so funny.

"Better load up, Jack," Wallace advised his brother. "This'll be your last home-cooked meal for a while."

Because his father was going to Japan.

Mark straightened up and blinked. He'd almost forgotten that soon he'd be there alone with Wallace and his family. Not that it upset him particularly. Especially since Susan and Wallace seemed so nice. Connie seemed okay for a girl, although Mark knew he'd have to wait to see if she turned out to be one of those clingy, leech-type little sisters who had to follow you around everywhere.

And that left Henry. So far he seemed okay. It had been fun going down to the beach with him and throwing stones out into the water. But still, there was something about Henry that struck Mark as being a little strange. He still remembered the look on his face when Susan said Mark could wear one of his winter jackets. And once or twice that afternoon he'd looked at Henry and felt a strange, eerie sensation, as if something wasn't quite right.

As if something was missing.

Mark had shaken it off, telling himself he was probably imagining things. On the way to Maine, he and his father had talked about what a stressful time it was, with his mother dying and Jack having to go away. His father had cautioned him to take it easy and not take anything too seriously. Sometimes in stressful situations, he'd said, your perceptions could be clouded. Things might not always be the way they seemed.

At the other end of the table, the adults were talking about Jack's upcoming trip. Susan looked down at the kids' end of the table for a moment and noticed that Connie was picking up the broccoli with her fingers.

"Use your fork, Connie," she said.

"But my fingers get more," Connie said.

"Keep it up and they won't be getting dessert," Susan replied.

Mark cut a piece of roast beef and started to chew it. He sort of liked the way Susan could be strict but could make a little joke at the same time. He liked her style and instinctively trusted her. He glanced again at Alice Davenport, wondering where she was going to fit into all this.

Thump! Suddenly Mark felt a sharp, throbbing pain

in his right shin. It was the kind of pain he'd once felt when he'd run into the edge of a heavy glass coffee table. He turned and stared at Henry, who stared right back with an open, innocent look. Mark knew Henry may look innocent, but he was the only one sitting close enough to deliver a kick like that.

Well, he wasn't going to let him get away with it. Mark swung his leg and kicked Henry right back. He thought Henry might grunt, or even start a fight, but the kid just closed his eyes for a second as if he was letting the pain wash through him. Then he opened his eyes and smiled.

Mark was little surprised, but he smiled back.

He felt as if he'd just passed a test. He'd proved he could stand the pain.

They were even. And it was their secret.

Henry started to giggle. Mark watched him uncertainly, then began to giggle as well. As the pain diminished, it did seem a little funny. Here at this fancy table with these adults, they'd both delivered hard kicks to each other's shin and no one had even noticed!

As the giggles grew louder, Alice Davenport noticed and put her hand on Jack's arm. Jack had been concerned about how Henry and Mark would get along, but it was becoming obvious that he had little to worry about. The boys seemed to be getting along fine.

After dinner Jack and Mark walked back out to the car. It was dark and cold, but Mark felt warmed by the meal he'd just had. He hated the thought of his father leaving.

"You sure you have to go tonight?" Mark asked. "Can't you at least stay until morning?"

"My plane leaves from Logan Airport at seven A.M.," his father replied. "I've got to drive down to

Boston tonight and stay in a hotel. Believe me, Mark, I'd stay here if I could."

Mark nodded quietly. They reached the car, and his father opened the door. But instead of getting in, he crouched down until he was at Mark's eye level.

"You understand why I have to go, don't you?" Jack asked.

Mark shrugged and nodded. Jack closed his hands around Mark's arms and pulled him close.

"I'm leaving you now so that I'll never have to leave you again," Jack said. "I'll be gone three weeks at the most. Maybe less."

Mark looked away. He knew his father had to go to Japan to save his business. He'd known it for almost a week. The weird thing was, when it came right down to going, Mark didn't want his father to leave. Not now. Not ever.

"You're worried I'm going to leave and not come back," Jack guessed. "You're worried you're going to be left with no one."

Mark nodded. "Like, what if your plane crashes or something?"

"Planes don't crash very often," Jack said. "There are literally thousands of flights every day."

"But, with our luck," Mark couldn't help muttering.

"They say lightning never strikes in the same place twice, Mark," his father said. "I know it's hard, but we've got to start looking toward the future."

"Sure," Mark said halfheartedly.

"Something else bothering you?" Jack asked.

"What's with that Alice lady?" Mark asked.

Jack nodded as if he'd expected something like that. "She's a psychologist."

"So?"

"So, with me being gone at such a critical time, Susan and I thought it might be a good idea if you had someone you could talk to," Jack explained. After meeting with Alice and speaking to her, Jack had come around to Susan's way of thinking. Alice impressed him as a caring and sympathetic person, who would be a good ear for Mark.

"But I don't even know her," Mark said.

Jack couldn't help smiling a little. "Sometimes that makes it easier."

It might have seemed that way to Jack, but not to Mark. "Well, I think I'd rather talk to you."

"That's not so easy," Jack said. "It's not only expensive to talk to Tokyo, but it's pretty much night there when it's day here."

"Then I'll wait until you get back," Mark said.

"Mark, please believe me, going to see her won't be such a big deal."

But the thought shocked Mark. "I actually have to go *see* her?"

"Well, sure." It was growing obvious to Jack that he'd assumed too much.

"At her house?" Mark asked.

"She has an office in her house," Jack said. "But it's not like going to the doctor. I mean, she's not going to give you a shot."

"But I still have to talk to her," Mark said. It wasn't as bad as getting a shot, but it was close.

"You do whatever you're comfortable doing," his father said. "If you want to go in there and just stare at her for forty-five minutes, do it. But it would make me feel better knowing that you were going to go."

Mark rolled his eyes.

"Hey, come on." Jack forced a smile on his face. "Cheer up. *It's winter break.* Except for going to see Alice, you don't have to do anything except play with Henry and have a great time until I get back."

Mark knew his father was only trying to make him feel better. It wouldn't do any good to make him feel worse. Besides, it was cold, and he was starting to shiver again.

"Hey, listen," Jack said. "You're going to be okay. You know how I know?"

Mark shook his head. His teeth began to chatter.

"I know you'll be okay because I believe in you," Jack said.

Mark nodded and shivered some more. Jack saw that his son was cold. He rubbed the material of Mark's jacket between his fingers.

"This isn't warm enough for around here," he said.

"It's okay, Dad, really," Mark said. "Susan said I could wear some of Henry's stuff."

Jack sighed and felt disappointed in himself. "Guess I won't be winning any awards for Father of the Year, will I?"

Mark hated to see his father get down on himself. It wasn't his fault Mark's jacket wasn't warm enough. He knew his father was trying his best. He threw his arms around his father's neck. "I love you, Dad."

"That's right," Jack said, hugging him back and fighting to keep the tears from falling out of his eyes. "Make it worse."

"I didn't mean to." Mark squeezed his father hard, not wanting to let go. Not wanting his father to see how close to crying he was.

"We'll be together again real soon," Jack whispered. "I promise. Now I have to drive down to Boston."

Jack slowly worked his way out of his son's arms. He slid into the car and pulled the door closed. He and Mark looked at each other through the window one last time, then he started the car and drove slowly down the driveway.

Mark watched the car roll away. He didn't move until the red taillights had turned out of the driveway and disappeared down the winding road along the ocean. Only then did he turn and look back at the house. The front door was open, and framed in the friendly light was Susan, waiting for him.

7

MARK WATCHED TV WITH HENRY AND CONNIE THAT night. Perhaps because she wanted to make Mark feel comfortable, or because school was out, Susan let them stay up late. By the time Mark and Henry went to bed in Henry's room, Mark was so tired he hardly paid any attention to the world around him. All he remembered was lying down in one bed and Henry getting into the other. He wasn't even sure he remembered the lights going out.

The next morning Mark woke up in a strange room filled with sunlight. For a moment he sat up and looked around, not at all sure where he was. Then it came back to him: He was in Henry's room.

But where was Henry? His bed was empty, the sheets and blankets left unmade. Mark slowly looked around the rest of the room. Along one wall was a long workbench, and on it were tools and a couple of half-taken-apart radios. Mark also spied a crossbow and two air guns, as well as a big chemistry set with some kind of experiment going on. But if there was one theme to the room, it was warfare. Here and there

45

were old army helmets, belts, a fold-up army shovel, and empty metal ammunition cans. Hanging on the walls were models of tanks, jet fighters, missiles, and submarines.

Mark got up and went to the window. Outside it was a sunny day. Henry was walking away from the house. Under one arm he appeared to be carrying some planks of wood. In the other hand Mark thought he saw a hammer and a saw.

Suddenly feeling that he didn't want to be left behind, Mark pulled open the window. The frosty winter air rolled in and chilled him, but he leaned out.

"Henry!" he called, watching his breath come out in a long plume of vapor.

Henry didn't seem to hear him.

"Henry!" Mark called more loudly. But it was no use. Henry kept on walking toward the woods, out of earshot.

Now shivering, Mark pulled the window closed and quickly pulled his clothes on. Moments later, he stepped out into the hallway and walked toward the stairs. As he passed an open doorway, he suddenly saw something that made him stop.

It was the room of a young boy. There was a small child's bed, a bookcase with picture books, and big colorful plastic toys a toddler might play with. But the thing about the room that was so arresting was how neat and untouched it was. It looked like a room in a museum. Everything was exactly where it should have been.

Then Mark remembered that there'd been another child: a boy who'd died. This must have been his room.

Mark turned away and started down the stairs two at a time as he pulled on his jacket. Just as he reached the bottom and headed for the front door, Susan stepped out into the entryway. She was wearing a floppy white sweater and jeans and had a big smile on her face.

"Not so fast, mister," she said. "I happen to take breakfast very seriously."

"But . . ." Mark glanced outside.

"No 'but's." Susan steered him into the kitchen. The round wooden kitchen table was set with glasses, dishes, and bowls. Boxes of Sugar Pops, Cheerios, and Frosted Mini-Wheats stood on the table, along with pitchers of milk and orange juice and a basket of breakfast rolls.

"I just happen to be making a batch of pancakes," she said, taking a large hot frying pan off the stove. "Or you have your choice of cereals."

Mark was far more interested in seeing where Henry was going than he was in eating breakfast, but he didn't want to be rude. "Pancakes would be great," he said.

Susan smiled and set a plate with two steaming pancakes down in front of him. "Care for some sausage?"

"Uh, no thanks," Mark said.

"How about some real Vermont maple syrup?"

"Uh, what's that?" Mark asked.

Susan looked surprised. "You've never had real Vermont maple syrup?"

Mark shook his head.

"You're in for a treat," Susan said. "This is the real thing, straight from the tree."

She poured the syrup over his pancakes. Mark dipped his fork in it and had a taste.

"What do you think?" Susan asked eagerly.

"Uh, it's good," Mark said. It tasted different from the syrup he'd tasted in places like the International House of Pancakes, but he still wasn't sure what the big deal was.

"This is made from real maple-tree sap," Susan said, gesturing to the small metal can of syrup. "The syrups you get in the store are just sugar, water, and food coloring."

Mark nodded and took a few bites. He felt as if Susan was hovering over him. When adults did that it sometimes bothered him, but he had to admit there was something a little soothing in knowing someone cared when he was all alone.

Susan sat down beside him and took his hand. She looked right into his eyes. "Everything's going to be okay, Mark," she said in a soothing voice. "You'll see."

Instead of looking away, Mark looked right back into her eyes. Just as he had the night before, he felt an odd sense of kinship with her.

"Mark! Hey, Mark!" It was Henry, calling from outside. Mark looked out the kitchen window and saw that he'd come back toward the house. Now he stood outside and waved. Mark gave Susan a pleading glance. She smiled and shook her head.

"Well, so much for breakfast," she said with a wink. "I'll see you at lunch."

"Thanks." Mark was up and out the door in no time. His feet had hardly hit the grass when he heard Henry shout his name again.

Suddenly something dark was sailing toward his face. Mark barely had time to put his hands up.

Smack! A football slammed into his hand. It wasn't a soft Nerf ball, either. It was a hard, leather football, and it stung when he caught it. If Mark hadn't put his hands up fast, it would have smashed right into his face.

Mark tucked the football under his arm and looked around for Henry. His sense of surprise was turning into anger.

"Hey! Great catch!" Henry shouted. He was smiling, looking pleased that Mark had caught the ball.
"Come on, hit me!"

Mark heaved the ball back at Henry with all his
might. The ball sailed hard and low.

"Ooof!" Henry gasped as he gathered it against his
stomach. There was a split second while Mark waited
to see if Henry would be angry, but he seemed
delighted and quickly waved Mark to go out for
another pass.

Mark started to run. It was like the kick the night
before. Like some kind of test where he had to prove
himself. Henry threw another pass, and Mark caught
it and threw it back. Once again, the anger quickly
faded.

Heaving the ball back and forth, they made their
way across the backyard toward the woods where
Mark had watched Henry go earlier. As they entered
the trees, Henry tucked the football under his arm and
waved for Mark to join him.

"I want to show you something," he said.

Mark jogged alongside Henry, feeling good that
he'd proved himself capable with a football and that
Henry thought he was important enough to want to
show him things.

"What is it?" Mark asked.

"You'll see."

They stopped at the base of a massive tree.
Mark had never been so close to one so wide at the
bottom or so tall. Hammered into the tree were
some short pieces of two-by-four that served as
steps until a climber could reach the first branches.
Lying on the ground near them were some of the
planks Mark had seen Henry carrying earlier that
morning, as well as the saw, the hammer, and some
nails.

"You scared of heights?" Henry asked.

"No," Mark said, although that wasn't exactly true.

"Good." Henry pointed upward. "See up there?"

Mark looked. Through the branches he could see something near the top of the tree. It looked like a small platform. Mark turned back to Henry, who was tying some planks together with cord. He slipped the hammer through his belt and put a handful of nails in his pocket. He slung the planks over his shoulder and tied the rope off so they wouldn't slip. Then he grabbed the first steps and started to climb.

"See you at the top," he said.

Mark watched him climb the wooden steps. Given a choice, Mark would have preferred staying on the ground. When Henry reached the lowest branches, he stopped and looked back down.

"Aren't you coming?" he asked.

Mark swallowed. It was another test. The last thing he wanted to do was appear chicken. "Sure."

He reached for the first two-by-four and pulled himself up. The truth was, he was nervous. There were no trees in Arizona that were this high, and if there had been, he probably would not have climbed them.

Mark reached the branches and kept climbing. It wasn't as hard as he'd imagined. The branches were pretty evenly spaced, and when there wasn't a branch Henry had hammered in another two-by-four to serve as a step.

Suddenly Mark stopped and looked down, surprised at how high up he was. The planks Henry had left at the base of the tree looked hardly bigger than Lincoln Logs. Above him, Henry had reached the platform and now lay on his stomach, looking over the edge back down at him.

A few minutes later, Mark reached the branches just below the platform. He grabbed another branch and planted his foot on a small one. He was just about to pull himself up onto the platform when there was a loud *crack!* and the branch supporting his foot snapped.

He was falling!

For one terrifying second Mark was certain he was going to die. In a desperate attempt to save himself, he threw up his hands to grab for anything. Suddenly he felt two hands go around his wrists.

He stared up and found Henry above him, his arms extended down over the edge of the platform, holding him.

He was the only thing between Mark and a certain death. Mark's heart was beating so fast he could feel it all over his body. Adrenaline and fear raced through him. He stared up into Henry's face, but the smile he was used to seeing was gone. Henry gazed back at him with an empty, almost disinterested look.

Mark grunted and kicked his feet, trying to find a branch. Looking down for a foothold, he saw for the first time how sickeningly high in the air he hung. In a flash, his head snapped back up as he stared pleadingly into Henry's eyes.

Henry's lips began to move: "If I let you go, do you think you could fly?"

He had to be joking, but Mark was so terrified he couldn't get an answer out of his throat. He was totally at Henry's mercy. The idea that Henry would let go was inconceivable, yet at the same time so terrifying that Mark wanted to cry out.

Just then Henry pulled him up. Mark managed to get a hand on the edge of the platform. His legs were still swinging freely in the air beneath him, but now as he pulled himself up, he felt Henry grab his shoulders and help.

A moment later Henry pulled Mark onto the platform and they both lay there, gasping for breath. Mark couldn't believe how close he'd come. He didn't know what to think about Henry letting him hang there and asking him that crazy question. Once again, it made him feel angry, but when he looked over at Henry, the boy gave him that charming smile. Then Henry began to laugh and took a swipe at Mark's knee as if it had all been a big joke.

There was something infectious about Henry's laugh, and soon Mark found himself laughing as well. He wasn't sure it was all *that* funny. Maybe it was just the relief of knowing he was safe. Or maybe he was laughing because he wanted to be accepted.

After a few moments, Henry rolled onto his knees and began to untie the cord from the boards he'd carried up. Mark also rose to his knees and looked around. The view was really spectacular: The tops of huge bare trees surrounded them, and in the distance Mark could see the tall white steeple of a church and a river curling through the hills. When he turned and looked in the other direction, the ocean spread out before him, huge and blue and endless.

Mark took a deep breath, as if inhaling the fresh Maine air for the first time. He really thought he could like it here.

"Take the hammer," Henry said.

"Huh?" For a second, Mark stared at him without comprehending.

"Take the hammer and nail this one," Henry said, gesturing to the hammer in his pocket. He was holding a plank against a branch. Mark now saw that the reason Henry had carried the planks up was to expand the size of the platform.

"Is this gonna be an observation platform?" Mark asked as he steadied a nail and hit it with the hammer.

"A treehouse," Henry said.

"With walls?" Mark asked.

"Walls, windows, a door, and a roof," Henry said.

It seemed like quite an ambitious project to Mark. He might have doubted that Henry could do it, but he remembered the workbench in Henry's room. It seemed as if Henry was pretty capable with his hands.

It took ten minutes to hammer the planks Henry had carried from the ground.

"Time to go back down," Mark's cousin said, easing himself over the edge of the platform and starting to climb down through the branches. Mark waited a moment and then followed him.

When he got down to the ground, he saw that Connie had arrived. Henry had started chasing his sister and was shouting at her: "Connie! Drop that right now!"

"I'm not hurting it!" Connie yelled.

Mark started to follow them, and then he noticed the short branch that had broken under his weight and almost cost him his life. He picked it up and looked it over. Oddly, it appeared that part of it had been cut with a saw. No wonder it had snapped so quickly. Mark heard a shout and looked up, tossing the branch aside. Henry had caught up to Connie and was holding her tightly as he pried his football out of her hands.

"I don't care what you're doing!" he shouted angrily. "I gave you a simple rule to obey, okay? I've told you a thousand times: You never, ever, touch any of my things. Whatever it is, if it's mine, you don't touch it. Get it?"

The football fell out of Connie's hands, but Henry continued to squeeze her hard.

"Let go of me!" she cried. "Mom! *Mom!*"

Henry finally let go and Connie ran away toward the house with tears running down her face. Henry picked up the football and punted it angrily into the sky.

Mark watched from nearby. Apparently Henry was very possessive when it came to his things.

8

LATER THEY WENT BACK TO THE HOUSE FOR LUNCH. MARK was certain Connie must have told her mother what Henry had done, but if Susan was angry about it, she didn't reveal anything.

After lunch Henry wanted to go back outside again. This time he and Mark walked much farther into the woods than before. Soon they crossed several roads, squeezed through a hole in an old wooden fence, and came to an old railroad yard. Beyond it was the backyard of an abandoned factory. They walked past the brown, rusted hulks of huge old machines and stopped several dozen yards from the factory building. High above the building's brick walls were huge windows made of hundreds of smaller, individual panes of glass.

Henry looked around, then reached down and picked up a rock.

"Watch this," he said, taking aim and hurling the rock. A split second later, it sailed through a window with a crash.

Mark felt a moment's hesitation, as if somewhere deep inside he questioned whether this was the right thing to do. But then Henry turned to him and raised an eyebrow, as if asking what he thought.

Another test.

"Wow!" Mark gasped. "Great throw!" If he'd felt some hesitation about what Henry had done, it quickly disappeared. After all, it was an old, abandoned factory. Nobody used it anymore.

"Try it," Henry replied.

Mark reached down, found a rock, and threw it hard. It too crashed through a window.

"Good one!" Henry cried. Another crash followed a moment later as he threw a second rock.

It wasn't long before the boys had lost themselves in an orgy of rock-throwing, smashing dozens of windows. Mark had never done anything like this before. The fact that it was just a little bit wrong only made it feel more exciting.

"Hey!" a distant shout jarred them back to reality. Mark and Henry quickly turned to see an older man in faded blue overalls waving his arms and running toward them.

"Time to go," Henry said, and he began to sprint away across the railyard. Mark followed close behind, frightened the man would catch them. He was quite relieved when he saw the hole in the fence ahead. Moments later he followed Henry through and jogged after him down a road.

"Think we lost him?" Mark asked.

"Sure, he's just a watchman," Henry replied. "He didn't even follow us through the fence."

"Did you know he'd be there?" Mark asked.

"Sometimes he is and sometimes he isn't," Henry said.

They slowed to a fast walk and followed a curve in the road. They were passing a crumbling stone wall. Mark looked over it and saw old tombstones among the underbrush and gnarled old trees. The tombstones were broad and flat and gray. Some were chipped and cracked, others leaned at angles as if they might fall over at any time.

Henry stopped at a rusted metal gate in the wall. "In here," he said.

Mark hesitated. "You sure?"

"Why not?" Henry scowled.

"Well, it's a cemetery."

Henry grinned. "The dead people aren't gonna chase us out."

They walked through the graveyard. Some of the tombstones were so old the writing on them wasn't even legible anymore. Henry walked right past them toward a round stone well with a wooden cover over it, but Mark stopped and tried to read some of the inscriptions. A group of five tombstones grouped tightly together caught his eyes. He crouched down and read them.

"Wow," he said. "This is a whole family with the same last name. They all died on September tenth, eighteen thirty-eight. It says something about a fire."

"I know," Henry said as he slid the cover off the well. "Neat, huh?"

Neat?

Mark wasn't so sure it was "neat." Sounded kind of sad, actually. But it had happened a long time ago.

Mark left the tombstones and joined Henry by the well. He watched as Henry reached into a cavity in the stone wall and pulled out an old green metal box.

"This is a secret place, okay?" Henry said as he started to open the box. "You have to swear never to tell anyone about it."

"Okay," Mark said.

Henry took a red and white pack of Marlboros and a rusty old lighter out of the box. Mark watched in amazement as his cousin put a cigarette in his mouth and then lit it with the lighter. Henry took a deep drag and exhaled the smoke. Then he offered the cigarette to Mark.

"No, thanks." Mark shook his head.

"Go on," Henry said, pushing the cigarette toward him.

Mark saw that it was a dare. That it was yet another test. But this was one he wasn't interested in taking.

"They give you cancer," he said.

"So what?" Henry replied. "You're gonna die anyway."

Mark stared at him, a little shocked. It seemed like a strange thing to say. Mark had never actually thought about the possibility of dying himself. There were one or two times, like at the tree that morning, when it had occurred to him that it might be possible. But it still wasn't something he ever thought about. Old people died. And grown-ups who got sick.

Like his mother.

Henry was still holding the cigarette toward him. Mark could feel his resistance failing. He wanted to be friends with Henry. He *needed* a friend.

Mark reached for the cigarette. One drag probably wouldn't hurt. Besides, the truth was that he'd always wondered what it tasted like. Everybody told you how bad they were, and yet people still smoked them. There had to be something to it.

Mark pressed the filter against his lips and tasted the tobacco. A wisp of warm cigarette smoke got into his nose and burned his nostrils. Slowly, tentatively, he took a drag.

The distasteful smoke in his lungs instantly caused Mark to cough violently. A nauseated feeling swept through him, and he was afraid for a moment that he might throw up.

Mark handed the cigarette back to Henry, who climbed up on the well wall and stood on the edge. Mark climbed up on the wall beside him. The well was a deep black hole, and he couldn't see the bottom. He knew that what he was doing was dangerous, but he'd already coughed on the cigarette and didn't want to seem like a total dweeb by chickening out.

"Did you see your mother after she was dead?" Henry suddenly asked.

The question was a little personal and painful, but Mark felt compelled to answer. "I wanted to, but they wouldn't let me."

Henry took another drag and flicked the cigarette into the well. Out of the corner of his eye, Mark watched the red ember disappear into the darkness below. He didn't hear it hiss.

"You should've made them let you look," Henry said. "It's very important. Nobody actually talks about death. That's why you have to investigate it. It's scientific."

The talk of death and his mother made Mark feel very uncomfortable.

"It doesn't seem scientific to me," he said, hoping Henry would drop it. He didn't like talking about his mother as dead. He didn't like *thinking* of his mother as dead.

"What did your mom look like the last time you saw her?" Henry asked.

Mark winced and looked up into his eyes. Henry looked back with almost no expression on his face. He wasn't grinning or leering or anything. It just seemed like he was curious. Still, Mark wished he wouldn't talk about it.

"She looked kind of pale," Mark replied reluctantly.

"Kind of pale?" Henry frowned. "When my kid brother Richard drowned in the bathtub, I got a real good look."

Mark felt his eyes widen. "He drowned?"

"He was completely blue," Henry said. "You

should have looked at your mother's eyes and lips and touched her skin to see what it felt like. You know, hot . . . cold . . . whatever."

Her eyes? Her lips?

Without wanting to, Mark pictured it for a second. His mother dead. Her open glassy eyes, her pale bloodless lips. No, it was awful, too awful. He forced the thought out of his head, angry that Henry had made him think of such things. "Don't talk about my mother anymore."

"Hey, don't get mad," Henry said. "I was just being scientific."

"Talk about something else," Mark said.

"And if I don't?" Suddenly Henry wouldn't back down.

Mark stared at him. This wasn't open for discussion. His mother was off limits, and he wanted to make sure Henry knew it.

"I'll slug you," Mark threatened.

Henry stared back at him, unwavering. "Try it. I'll throw you down *there.*" He nodded down at the black hole below them.

The next thing he knew, Mark had raised his clenched fists. His emotions were a swirling rage inside him. He almost didn't care about the well—or anything else, for that matter. He just didn't want Henry to talk about his mother anymore.

Henry raised his fists. For a moment the boys just stared at each other. There was something so still and empty about Henry's eyes.

Henry dropped his fists and smiled sheepishly. "Hey, look, I'm sorry. That was real dumb of me. I know how I'd feel if I lost my mom. Friends?"

Mark watched as Henry extended his hand. Once again he felt his anger drain away. When Henry smiled and acted friendly like that, it was almost impossible not to like him. Mark unclenched his fists and offered his hand to Henry.

They shook. Mark wondered if Henry might try to do something funny, like give his hand a little pull, pretending to yank him off balance and into the well. But Henry let go of his hand and hopped down.

A moment later he was acting as though nothing had ever happened.

They spent the whole afternoon outside, sliding around on an ice-covered pond in their sneakers, climbing more trees, and throwing rocks at lined-up empty beer cans. Every time Mark thought there was nothing left to do, Henry always came up with something new and fun.

By late afternoon, the sun had begun to throw a pinkish light on the few clouds in the sky. Henry had yet another idea and checked his watch.

"Hey," he said, "it's time for the afternoon train!"

He began to run.

"We going somewhere?" Mark asked, running after him.

"You'll see," Henry said. "Got any pennies?"

"I think so. Why?"

"Just get 'em out," Henry said.

They raced across a field, then up an embankment and through a hole in a rusty old chain-link fence. They came across some railroad tracks on an elevated bed of gravel. Mark looked in both directions, but there was no sign of a train.

"You sure one's coming?"

"It doesn't always," Henry said. "But sometimes it does. Here, give me two pennies."

Mark reached into his pocket and took out two pennies. Henry put one on each rail. Then he got down on his hands and knees and pressed his ear against one of the rails.

"What are you doing?" Mark asked.

"Listening for the train," Henry said. He picked his head up and pressed his hand against his ear. "Wow, that's cold."

Mark smiled. "Did you hear one?"

"No, but let's wait awhile."

Mark took a step back down from the rails, but Henry just stood there beside the tracks. Mark knew Henry would have plenty of time to get away once they saw a train coming, but it still made him uneasy to see Henry standing there. He glanced up into the sky. The few wispy clouds had gone from light pink to a deeper color, and in the absence of sunlight he began to feel the chill of the coming evening.

"Here it comes!" Henry said.

Mark turned and saw that Henry had put his ear to the rail again. Mark looked far down the tracks but could see nothing. Henry really amazed him sometimes. He knew about all this stuff Mark had never been aware of. As Mark stared down the tracks, he now saw the glimmer of a light appear. Henry was right: The train was coming.

Mark backed down from the railroad bed a safe distance away, but Henry stayed on the tracks. Again Mark felt uneasy, but he knew Henry had plenty of time. Maybe he was showing off, or maybe he just felt as though he didn't have to get away from the tracks yet. Mark was tempted to say something, but he didn't want to seem like he was a scaredy cat or anything, so he picked up a stone and threw it back against the fence.

The train was coming closer. Henry had not yet left the tracks. What was he doing? Mark wondered.

Now the train was less than two hundred yards away. The whistle blew loudly. Henry walked down and joined Mark, but he took his time. The train whistle blew again, and on the tracks the pennies had begun to vibrate slightly.

Moments later the train rushed past, pulling a violent wake of wind. Henry couldn't have been more than ten feet from the tracks when the train hurled by. Even Mark, standing forty feet away, felt his hair being blown to the side. He closed his eyes as the air was filled with dust and a few brown slivers of torn leaves.

It was a freight train, but not a long one. After the locomotive, half the cars were boxcars and half were open log carriers, probably carrying logs away from some logging grounds to a paper mill.

The caboose had just passed when Henry scampered back up to the tracks and started searching around. In no time he'd found the two pennies, now both flattened paper-thin and shaped a little like guitar picks.

"Here you go," Henry said, flipping one of the flattened pennies to Mark. Mark caught it and was surprised.

"Wow, it feels hot!"

"Yeah, it has something to do with all the molecules getting moved around," Henry said.

Mark grinned and pocketed the penny. He was amazed by some of the things his cousin knew. He and Henry started to walk along the top of the rails, with their arms out for balance, like tightrope walkers.

"Hey, Mark," Henry said. "You know this song?" He began to sing: "Great big gobs of greasy, grimy gopher guts . . ."

"Mutilated monkey meat," Mark joined in, and they sang the rest together: "Chopped-up little piggies' feet. French-fried eyeballs swimming in a pool of blood. Mmmm, that sure tastes good. . . ."

Still walking the rails, they laughed out loud, then started the song again.

They were home just before dark and had dinner with Wallace, Susan, and Connie. Mark found himself gradually letting his guard down. He felt comfortable with this family. Even though he and Henry had had some tense moments, Mark pretty much passed it off to a feeling-out process you had to go through with any new friend.

After dinner they watched TV until Susan said it was time for bed. Mark and Henry went upstairs and washed up and got into their beds. They lay in bed and talked for a while about Henry's plans for the treehouse, then Susan stopped in the doorway and flicked off the light.

The room went dark, except for the shaft of hallway light coming through the doorway.

"Okay, you guys, time to sleep," Susan said. "See you in the morning."

She left the door partially open. Mark yawned. His eyelids felt heavy, and he did feel tired. It had been a long day, and he and Henry had covered a lot of ground. He lay on his back, his head sinking into the soft feather pillow and his eyes closed.

"Hey, Mark?" Henry whispered.

Mark opened his eyes. "Yeah?"

"Great big gobs of greasy, grimy gopher guts," Henry whispered.

Mark grinned.

"Mutilated monkey meat," Henry whispered.

Mark giggled.

"Chopped-up little piggies' feet."

They both giggled.

"All right, boys." Wallace stood in the partly open doorway. "Knock it off."

Both Henry and Mark stopped giggling—for a second. Then the giggling resumed.

"I mean it," Wallace said, although Mark could sense that he was halfhearted about it.

Mark and Henry both made noises as if they were suppressing laughter.

"Now that's it," Wallace said. "I don't want to hear one more *peep.*"

"Peep," Henry squeaked. Mark couldn't help giggling. In the doorway Wallace shook his head and smiled, then walked away.

"Peep, peep, peep." Henry sounded like a little frog. Mark had to press his face into his pillow to muffle his laughter. It had been a long time since he'd had this much fun.

It grew quiet in the room again. Mark rolled over and looked at Henry's dark silhouette in the bed.

"Henry?" Mark said quietly.

"Yeah?"

"Today was fun."

"Yeah," Henry said.

Again it was quiet. Mark started to roll away.

"Hey, Mark?" Henry said.

Mark rolled back and stared through the dark at him.

"Yeah?"

"Tomorrow's gonna be even better."

9

THE NEXT MORNING AFTER BREAKFAST, HENRY WANTED to go back to the railroad tracks.

"Are we gonna put more pennies on the tracks?" Mark asked. He actually hoped they weren't. It had been fun yesterday, but it seemed a little dumb to do it again today.

"Nope, something better," Henry replied.

They walked across the field and through the hole in the chain-link fence. This time when they came to the tracks, Henry started to walk them again, heading for a railroad trestle several hundred yards away.

A few minutes later, in the shadow of the trestle, Henry stared to scan the ground.

"What are you looking for?" Mark asked.

"You'll see," Henry replied. He looked around a few moments more and then reached down for something that was half buried in the gravel. He pulled up a rusty railroad spike.

"Help me find more," Henry said.

"What for?"

"You'll see. Come on, let's see who can find the most."

66

Mark began to look around on the ground. Like the first one Henry had found, most of the spikes were partly buried. Sometimes only a little bit of the end showed through. Once Mark got used to what to look for, he started finding them without difficulty.

Soon their pockets were bulging with the heavy spikes.

"If I find any more I think my pockets will rip," Mark said.

Henry nodded and patted his own pockets. "Yeah, that's enough for now. Let's go."

"Where?"

"You'll see."

Once again Mark started to follow Henry. He wasn't sure why Henry always had to make a mystery of things, never telling Mark anything more than was necessary. But in a way, Mark didn't mind. Never knowing what was coming next did make it feel like more of an adventure.

Walking with their pockets filled with spikes wasn't easy. It was more like waddling. They followed the tracks for a while, and then Henry turned through another hole in the fence. This one led through some woods toward a large pond. The pond was wide and partly covered by ice, and Henry and Mark began to walk along it. Soon they came to a long, narrow footbridge that went across the pond. It was just wide enough for a person to walk across.

Henry started across it and Mark followed. Below them the pond lay still and unmoving.

"Grrrr . . . Rooof! Rooof!" The explosive, angry barks of a dog startled them. Henry and Mark quickly spun around. A large brown-and-white dog was racing through the woods toward them, its teeth bared.

Mark turned to Henry, whose eyes had gone wide with fear. There was no doubt in Mark's mind that this was a part of the adventure his cousin hadn't bargained on.

"Nice knowing you!" Henry gasped and started to run. Mark raced after him. For a second he forgot about the heavy spikes in his pockets, but as they clinked and rubbed against his legs he was quickly reminded.

Not only did they slow him down, but Mark suddenly realized that his pants were starting to slip down on his hips. He quickly grabbed his belt and pulled them up.

"Grrrr . . . Rooof! Roof!" The dog raced up behind them. Ahead, Mark spotted a gate at the other end of the bridge. If they could just make it . . .

"Ahhh!" Mark suddenly stumbled and fell, banging his knees painfully against the wooden planks of the bridge's floor. Quickly rising to his hands and knees, he looked back.

As if surprised he'd fallen, the dog also stopped. For one moment Mark's and the dog's eyes met. Then the dog snarled and charged forward.

Mark felt a hand grab his collar and pull him up. He turned and looked into Henry's face as his cousin helped him to his feet and pushed him ahead. Once again the race was on.

Mark made it through the gate. Henry was right behind, slamming the gate behind him just as the dog crashed into it.

"Grrrr . . . Roooof! Roooof!" With its paws on top of the gate, the dog howled angrily.

On the other side of the gate, the boys stumbled to the ground and sat there exhausted, gasping for breath.

"Wow," Mark said between deep breaths. "That was close."

"These spikes slowed us down," Henry said, patting his bulging pockets.

"Yeah." Mark nodded. "I really thought we were gonna be Gaines Burgers. Thanks for helping me up."

Henry smiled and then laughed, but the barking of the dog drowned him out. He and Mark got to their feet. Mark turned to go, then realized that Henry had turned in the other direction—back toward the dog.

"What are you doing?" Mark asked.

Henry didn't answer. As he stepped closer to the gate, the dog barked more ferociously. Even though the gate appeared strong, Mark couldn't imagine getting that close to the dog again. Yet Henry walked silently toward the gate and just stood there, barely a foot from the crazed animal.

"Henry?" Mark said softly. Again there was no reply. Mark wasn't even sure Henry had heard him. His cousin just stood on the other side of the gate and stared—eyes narrowed and his own teeth bared—back at the dog.

To Mark's amazement, the dog stopped barking. For several moments boy and dog just stared at each other, as if it was some kind of contest or battle of wills.

"Uh, Henry?" Mark said nervously. "Come on, let's go."

Henry didn't move. He and the dog were dead silent, their eyes fixed on each other. Mark couldn't understand it. He'd never seen anyone do anything like that. It was creepy.

The dog's ears went down and his mouth slowly closed. He hung his head, slid back down from the fence, and slowly walked away with his tail between his legs.

Henry turned and grinned at Mark. The intense, fierce look was gone. Henry acted as if nothing had happened.

"Are you okay?" Mark asked in wonder.

"Huh?" Henry looked puzzled. "Of course I am. Uh, did you say something before?"

"I said, let's go."

"Yeah." Henry's smile broadened and his eyes brightened with new excitement. "Let's go. I want to show you something cool."

Once again they headed off through the woods. Mark still felt disturbed by the incident he'd just witnessed, but the memory started to fade as they walked along, their pockets still weighed down with the spikes.

Soon they came to some cliffs high above the ocean. Two hundred feet below they could see the waves crashing on the rocks. They started to walk toward the edge of the cliff. Here and there a gnarled old tree stood by itself, braving the elements. Mark stopped a few feet from the lip, but Henry kept on walking until he stood right on the edge. The toes of his sneakers actually hung out over the cliff.

Henry looked back over his shoulder and smiled at Mark.

"Come on," he said. "I thought you weren't afraid of heights."

Another test. Mark felt a little disappointed. He thought he'd passed all the tests. Now here was another one, and in some ways, the worst yet. But how could he say no? They'd been having so much fun.

"Okay." Mark took a deep breath and stepped forward. His stomach started to churn nervously. A moment later he inched the tips of his tennis shoes out over the edge and stood level with Henry. He stared out at the place on the horizon where the water met the sky and felt the breeze lifting his hair. Were a strong gust to blow from behind, it might tip him right over the edge. The thought sent a chill through him.

"Look down," Henry said.

Without really knowing why, Mark looked down.

The drop was dizzying. It was hundreds of feet straight down to the waves crashing on the rocks below. Mark began to feel weak in the knees.

"Close your eyes," Henry said.

"Why?" Mark asked.

"Because it's a great feeling."

Mark closed his eyes. Suddenly it was impossible to judge the strength of the breeze or to have a sense of what was level. Mark felt himself leaning forward. His arms shot out reflexively, and his eyes burst open. He'd started to lose his balance. For a brief instant he was certain he was going to fall.

Then his forward motion stopped.

Henry had grabbed his shirt. Now he pulled him back from the edge. Thrown off balance by the bolts in his pockets, Mark stumbled a few steps and then straightened.

"You okay?" Henry asked.

"Sure, I'm fine," Mark replied. But his forehead felt hot, and a faint feeling rushed through him as he thought about how close he'd just come.

To dying.

"Let's go." Henry began to walk along the cliff. Mark walked alongside him, telling himself that he wasn't going to succumb to any more of Henry's tests.

They walked along the cliff, looking out at the ocean. A flock of white birds circled in the air and dove into the water. In the distance, a lobster boat rose and fell in the ocean swells.

Suddenly Mark saw something ahead of them. Standing on a part of the cliff that jutted out toward the ocean was someone wearing a white sweater and jeans. As Mark got closer, he could see that it was Susan, standing with her back to them, staring out at the ocean.

"Isn't that your mom?" Mark asked.

"Yeah," Henry said. "She's always out there."

"Why?"

"She goes there to think about Richard," Henry said. "Kind of weird, huh? Come on, I want to show you my new invention."

Henry turned to the right and started to walk faster.

"Why don't we go say hello?" Mark asked.

"Nah."

"Come on," Mark said.

Henry stopped and looked back at his mother. He shook his head. "She likes to be alone when she comes out here."

He started walking again. Mark lingered behind, staring at his aunt. It was strange to see her standing out there like that. Stranger still was the way Henry wanted to avoid her.

"Hey, come on."

Mark turned and saw that Henry had stopped a dozen yards away and was waving to him. Mark nodded, took one last look at Susan, and headed toward him.

Henry led Mark back to the garage that stood beside the house.

"Velcome to my la-*bor*-atory," Henry said, holding the side door open and imitating Count Dracula.

Mark stepped into the garage. It was dark and cluttered with all kinds of junk. Obviously there was no room for a car. Instead, the floor was covered with partly dismantled lawnmowers and broken toaster ovens. Here was an old record player, and over there a large model airplane with a broken wing.

Henry walked over to a workbench covered with tools and pulled on a string light switch. Above them a pair of fluorescent lights flickered on, and Mark saw that standing in the middle of the workbench was something covered by a sheet of dark plastic. With a dramatic sweep, Henry pulled off the sheet to reveal some kind of mechanical device.

"Ta-dah!" Henry took a bow.

Mark took a closer look. The machine looked like some kind of miniature catapult, with pair of heavy springs on either side and a slot down the middle.

"What does it do?" Mark asked.

"I'll show you." Henry grunted as he picked up the heavy device and headed for the door.

"Where are we going?" Mark asked.

"The testing grounds," Henry answered. He turned back to Mark. "See that ratchet lying on the table?"

Mark turned back and saw a long chrome tool with a rounded end. "This?"

"Yeah," Henry said. "Bring it along. We'll need it."

They went back outside. Henry walked slowly, lugging the heavy device down the driveway and across the street. They walked about a hundred yards down the road, which was lined by a low stone wall.

Finally Henry stopped and placed the device on the wall.

"Okay, here," he said, climbing over the wall and gesturing for Mark to follow him.

Moments later they were crouched on the other side of the wall as Henry lined up the machine.

"Incredible, huh?" he said. "It took me a long time to find all the parts."

"You made this yourself?" Mark asked in amazement.

"You better believe it," Henry replied.

"How?" Mark asked.

"What do you mean, how?" Henry asked.

"Like, did you follow instructions or something?"

Henry grinned. "Yeah, but they came from up here." He pointed to his head.

It was difficult for Mark to believe that anyone his age could build such a thing out of spare parts, but he'd never seen anything like the device before. It appeared to be something original.

"You got that ratchet?" Henry asked, holding out his hand.

"Here." Mark pulled it out of his pocket and handed it to him.

Henry attached the ratchet to a spot on the side of the device and began to work it back and forth.

"See these big springs?" he asked. "They're so strong I have to use this to cock them."

The ratchet made a clicking sound as Henry worked it back and forth. The catapult part slowly went back as the springs stretched and creaked.

"Now, when they're all the way back," Henry said, "you can load the spike here."

Mark watched as he took one of the railroad spikes from his pocket and slid it into the slot. So that was why they'd collected them.

Henry adjusted the device, and Mark realized he was aiming it at something across the road. Looking over, he saw a cat sitting on the wall on the other side of the road. Henry lined up the device and then pulled the ratchet a few more times until the springs were stretched as far back as they could go.

The cat wasn't even aware of them. It was just sitting on top of the wall, licking its paws. Mark began to get a funny feeling in the pit of his stomach.

"You're not going to try to hit it, right?" he said. "You're just gonna give it a good scare."

"Lock and load," Henry said, flipping a piece of metal over the railroad spike.

Once again, Henry squatted behind the device and adjusted its position.

"Now we line up kitty cat," he whispered.

"You're not gonna hit it, okay?" Mark whispered back.

There was a *clack!* as the springs snapped forward and the device fired.

Thwack! Across the road, just inches above the cat's

74

head, the spike sank into the trunk of a large tree. The cat's head shot up. It looked around for a moment, saw nothing to feel threatened by, and went back to licking itself.

"Cool!" Mark shouted.

He and Henry hopped over the wall and ran toward the cat. In a flash, the animal scampered away. The boys reached the tree and stared at the spike.

"Wow, it must have gone in almost three inches!" Mark gasped.

He grabbed the end of the spike and tried to pull it out. The spike wouldn't budge. It was embedded too deep.

"Incredible!" Mark yelled. "I can't believe the speed of the thing. I never even saw it go!"

Henry stood behind him, quietly surveying the scene. The cat had stopped thirty feet away and was staring back at them.

"The sight's not right yet," Henry said, shaking his head in disgust.

Mark looked up at him and followed his eyes to the cat.

"You're kidding, right?" he said. "You really weren't aiming at it, were you?"

Henry turned to him, and a small smirk creased his lips.

"Come on, we better go back," he said.

10

THE MOMENT MARK HAD BEEN DREADING ARRIVED. He and Henry had just finished lunch when Susan turned from the kitchen counter and said, "I almost forgot, Mark. Your appointment's at two."

"My appointment?" Mark didn't follow.

"With Alice Davenport."

Mark felt a little embarrassed that Susan had brought it up in front of Henry and Connie. Susan must have sensed that, because she said, "Connie, Henry, why don't you two go off and do something for a little while?"

Connie got up and left. Henry was slower to depart. "Have fun," he said to Mark.

A moment later, Mark and Susan were left alone in the kitchen.

"Maybe we should call up and cancel it," Mark said, bringing his dishes to the sink.

"Why?" Susan asked, as she ran the disposal unit. It sucked some apple cores and eggshells down with a loud slurping sound.

"I don't know," Mark said. "I guess I really don't feel like I need it."

Susan started to run the water and rinse the dishes before putting them in the dishwasher. "Your father set up the appointment, Mark. I know he really wants you to go."

"But things have changed," Mark said.

Susan looked surprised. "They have?"

"Well, sort of," Mark said. "I mean, I feel okay here. I don't really feel like I have to go talk to a stranger."

"I'm glad you feel that way, and I understand your reluctance," Susan said. "But I know you promised your father you'd go. And I promised him that I'd make sure you did."

"Do I have to?" Mark asked plaintively.

"It's not as bad as going to the dentist," Susan said.

Mark nodded, defeated. "I know, I know. She's not going to give me a shot."

Alice Davenport lived just outside of town. Susan offered to give Mark a ride, but there was plenty of time and Mark told her he'd just as soon walk.

"You sure you're going to go?" Susan gave him a skeptical look. It was funny, but somehow it reminded him of a certain look his own mother used to give him when he said he was going to do something and she wasn't certain if he really would.

"Yeah, don't worry, I'll really go."

Susan smiled at him. At least she was honest. Mark was glad she didn't try to pretend that she wasn't thinking he might ditch the appointment.

"Okay, Mark," she said. "I'll tell you how to get there."

Half a dozen times during the walk, Mark thought about turning around and going off in a different direction. He could always say he got lost. But he didn't. It was just his luck to have been brought up honest.

He knew why he was dreading the appointment. It wasn't that he was afraid of talking to Alice Davenport. He just didn't want to talk about his mother. He didn't want to have to think about what had happened. And he definitely didn't want to hear another adult tell him about how he had to face reality.

Mark reached a white picket fence. Ahead he could see a big white house on a point of land overlooking the bay. The morning breeze had died down, and smoke curled lazily upward from its stone chimney. Mark stopped and looked back. The walk had been gradually uphill, and behind him he could see the small quaint town of Rock Harbor nestled in the gray leafless woods.

He followed the fence to a gate that opened to a slate walk leading up to the house. Stopping at the gate, he gazed up at the house again. The truth was, he really, really, didn't want to go. If only there was some excuse he could think of to get out of it.

He must have stood at the gate for a long time. Suddenly the door to the house opened and Alice Davenport stepped out and waved. She was wearing a red corduroy dress with pockets, and she was holding a mug.

"Just lift the latch," she said easily, as if pretending the reason he'd stood there for so long was that he couldn't figure out how to open the gate.

Mark opened the gate and let himself in. He felt very self-conscious walking up the path with Alice watching him. As if she knew this, she turned back into the house, leaving the door open.

Mark stepped into the house and closed the door behind him. Unlike Wallace's house, which was a little dark and somber and wood-paneled, Alice Davenport's house was filled with bright colors. The walls were yellow and lined with large pastel paintings of desert scenes. Even the doorways were painted in pastel pinks and light blues.

"I'm in here, Mark," Alice called.

Mark looked through a doorway to his right. He couldn't see Alice, but inside was a small waiting room with a couch and a lamp and a pile of magazines on a coffee table.

"Would you mind closing the door behind you?" Alice asked.

Mark stepped into the waiting room and closed the door. Now he could see the office. It was painted white, with colorful abstract paintings on the walls. Alice was sitting at a wooden desk with some books and papers on it. Behind her was a large picture window looking out over the bay.

"You can come in, Mark," she said.

Mark stepped into the office. Now he could see some low shelves along one wall, filled with children's games and toys. There was a couch in the room and a chair. Mark glanced at Alice quizzically.

"Whichever you'd like," Alice said.

Mark chose the chair.

"So, how are you?" Alice asked.

"Fine."

"Are you enjoying your stay at your uncle's?"

"Yes."

"I'm glad."

Mark nodded, but he didn't really care that she was glad. Instead of asking another question, Alice just sat quietly and looked at him. Mark felt uncomfortable. He didn't want to look back. Glancing over at the shelves, he noticed a toy kaleidoscope.

Again he glanced at Alice.

"Go right ahead," Alice said.

Mark reached over and picked up the toy. He aimed it out the window and turned it slowly, making all kinds of designs.

Minutes passed. Mark occupied himself with the kaleidoscope. Finally Alice cleared her throat.

"You know, this is a nice change," she said. "Most of the people who come see me . . . all they want to do is talk."

Her tone was warm and humorous, but Mark wasn't fooled.

"I'm not dumb, you know," he muttered.

"What?" Alice asked curiously.

"You think you can get me to talk by acting like you don't want me to," Mark said. "You're using reverse psychology."

"I can't help it," Alice replied without missing a beat. "I'm a reverse psychologist."

It was actually kind of funny. Mark almost smiled, then caught himself. "Well, I just don't have anything to say."

"Your dad thinks you do," Alice said.

"Then maybe he should come here."

Alice didn't respond. She just gazed at him with a sympathetic look on her face. Now Mark felt bad for being fresh.

"Well, he just wants me to talk about my mom," he said.

"I know," Alice replied.

"And like I said, I have nothing to say."

Alice nodded slowly. "Mark, when we lose someone we love—"

"I can handle it," Mark quickly cut her off. He didn't want to get a lecture. That was the *last* thing he wanted.

"Can you?" Alice asked.

Mark took a deep breath and let it out slowly. "I have to."

"Why?"

"Because when you do something . . . " he began. It was hard to explain. He didn't really want to explain.

It was a secret he'd been harboring since his mother died. It was his problem. Something he had to work on himself. Yet at the same time, he realized that it was something that wanted to come out.

"Yes? . . ." Alice nudged him gently. Against his will, Mark could feel the thing he didn't want to say pushing its way out.

"It's just that when something's your fault . . ." The words trailed off. Why was he talking about this? Why couldn't he keep it to himself?

"What did you do?" Alice asked.

"I . . . I let someone die," Mark blurted out. The words felt as if someone else had spoken them. He couldn't believe he'd said that. He wasn't even sure he'd ever thought of it precisely that way before, but as soon as he heard himself say it, he knew that it was true. That was how he felt. That was the thing he'd been keeping locked inside.

He'd told his mother he wouldn't let her die.

And then he had.

Across the room, Alice didn't look surprised or shocked or anything like that. She just leaned forward and held him with her eyes. "Tell me how you did it," she said softly. "Tell me how you let your mother die."

Before Mark could stop himself, the words came spilling out.

The dam had broken.

The wind kicked up again around dinnertime, and increased into the evening. Outside, the bare brown branches swayed and creaked as the wind whistled through them. In the bedroom he shared with Henry, Mark twisted restlessly in his sheet and blanket.

Someone was calling him. "Mark? Mark, can you hear me?"

It was his mother!

Mark looked around. He was in the woods. "Mom?"
he shouted. "Where are you?"

"Here, Mark," came the reply.

But all Mark saw were trees moving, turning slowly
as if inside a kaleidoscope.

"I can't see you!" he shouted.

"I'm here." But now even her voice was kaleidoscop-
ic, coming from eight directions at once.

"Which one are you?" he cried.

"This one ... this one ... this one ... this one
... this one ..."

"Which one?" he cried.

"Which one? Which ..." Mark's eyes opened.
What now? Where were the trees? How had it gotten
to be so dark all of a sudden?

"Mom?" he said.

Outside, the wind whistled in response. Mark
looked over at the dark shape of Henry asleep in his
bed.

It was a dream. Just a dream.

Or was it?

Mark heard a faint creak, and the door to Henry's
room opened a few inches. A shaft of light from the
hall spilled in.

Who'd opened the door? Was it the wind?

Suddenly someone passed by in the hall. Mark had
only a glimpse but he could tell it was a woman.

In a white dress.

Like the dress in his mother's closet.

"Mom?" Mark whispered. No, it wasn't possible.
Or was it?

There was no answer. But it sure looked like her.
Maybe it was her. Maybe she'd come back because
he'd talked so much about her that afternoon. . . .

Mark climbed out of bed and walked barefoot
across the room. He pulled open the door and looked

out. The hallway was empty. Where could she have gone?

He walked out to the top of the stairs and looked down. Suddenly he felt his heart leap into his throat. There she was! In the white dress. She'd gone downstairs. Her back was toward him as she stopped by a small table and pulled open a drawer beneath it.

"Mom? . . ." Mark couldn't believe it. He started down the stairs gently and slowly, as if afraid to frighten her. As if a loud noise might cause her to bolt away like a startled rabbit. Just a few steps from the bottom, one of the steps creaked.

His mother heard it and turned around.

Only it wasn't his mother.

It was Susan.

Mark's hopes fell like a wave on a beach and crashed. His legs gave out and he sat down hard on the steps.

How could it not be her? He'd been certain it was her. How could it be Susan?

His aunt stared back at him with a concerned look on her face. "Mark?"

It had to be her. It just couldn't not be her.

"Mark, what's the matter, honey?" Susan asked, taking a step toward him.

Mark just stared at her. He could feel his lower lip tremble and his eyes begin to fill with tears. Maybe it was her. Maybe she'd just . . . *changed* a little.

All those things Susan did that were just like the things his mother did. The way she was soft and nice and understanding.

Yes. His mother was there, somewhere.

Inside of Susan.

"Mark?" Susan's expression went from concern to outright worry.

"It is you," Mark whispered. "You came back. I knew you'd come back."

Susan stared at him, not quite comprehending. "I didn't go anywhere. I've been right here all the time."

It was too much. Just as the words had come spilling out to Alice Davenport, now all the grief Mark had been holding inside came spilling out. Mark buried his face in his hands and began to sob. All the pain and misery of the past year, ever since his mom had gotten sick . . . It all came pouring out.

He felt Susan come closer, felt her arms slide around him, but it made no difference. Nothing on the outside mattered. It was all on the inside, and it was all pouring out.

Susan held the boy in her arms and rocked him gently. She knew it wasn't enough to soothe him, but it was all that she could do.

The sound of a boy crying brought Wallace out of the den. He stood in the doorway at the end of the hall, not wanting to let his presence be noticed.

Someone else watched them as well. At the top of the landing Henry stood in his pajamas, watching how his mother cradled Mark, and how his father stood in the doorway silently.

Why was his mother doing that?

She was *his* mother, not Mark's. He wished she'd stop.

11

IN THE MORNING, HENRY'S BED WAS EMPTY AGAIN. MARK was slow to get up. He hadn't gotten much sleep the night before. All those feelings . . . all that crying . . . Just the memory of it made him feel tired.

Finally he got up and went to the window. There was no sign of Henry out in the yard. Mark got dressed and went downstairs.

Susan was in the kitchen. Mark went in and sat at the table, facing away from her. Feeling shy and a little embarrassed about the night before, he avoided her gaze. He wondered why she'd put on that white dress and where she'd gotten it from, but he couldn't bring himself to ask.

Then he heard the soft padding of her footsteps and knew she was coming closer. He felt a hand rest gently on his shoulder.

"How are you feeling?" she asked.

"Okay." Mark glanced up for a second. He saw caring and concern in her eyes and no longer felt quite so embarrassed.

She cared. She understood.

Just like his mom.

Her hand left his shoulder, as if she knew just how long he'd be comfortable with it there.

"Hungry?"

"Yeah."

"What would you like this morning?"

Mark turned and his eyes met hers. "How about pancakes again? With *real* maple syrup?"

Susan smiled back. "You got it."

He was just finishing breakfast when Connie came in. This morning her blond hair fell loose to her shoulders and she was wearing a sweater and jeans, just like her mother. She regarded Mark shyly for a second, then crossed the kitchen and gestured for Susan to bend down. When Susan did, Connie whispered something in her ear.

Susan straightened up. "I don't know. Why don't you ask him?"

"Mom . . ." Connie whined a little.

"Go ahead, he doesn't bite."

Mark was dabbing his lips with a paper napkin. Connie came toward him, twirling the ends of her hair nervously in her fingers.

"Would you like to do a puzzle with me?" she asked.

"Would I like to do a puzzle with you?" Mark pretended to be surprised. He looked past the little girl's shoulder at Susan, who smiled. "Sure, I'll do a puzzle with you."

Connie's eyes widened, and a smile of delight crossed her face. "Okay, come on!"

The next thing Mark knew, she was pulling him by the hand into the living room. In front of the couch was a square, flat, wooden coffee table.

"You wait here," Connie told him. "I'll be right back."

Mark waited while the little blond girl hurried out of the room. In almost no time she was back with a box. It was a colorful jigsaw puzzle of a pony in a grassy field.

Connie opened the box and spilled the pieces out. They were twice the size of the pieces in a regular jigsaw puzzle.

"What should we do first?" Connie asked.

"Well, I always turn all the pieces over so I can see every one," Mark told her.

They turned the pieces so that they were all facing up.

"Can we do the pony first?" Connie asked.

"Good idea," Mark said. "It should be easy, because it's the only part of the puzzle that's brown."

Connie gathered all the brown pieces, but she still had some difficulty putting the pony together. Mark patiently gave her hints until she finished that part.

"You did it, Connie! That's great!" Mark acted as though she'd just performed some miracle. Connie beamed.

"What should we do next?" she asked.

"Well, I always like to do the outside," Mark said. "All the pieces with a straight edge." Mark picked a few pieces out and put them together to set an example.

But Connie frowned.

"What's wrong?" Mark asked.

"It's too hard that way," the little girl said.

"Okay, then pick another color."

"Let's do the sky," Connie said, and she started piecing together the light-blue pieces. She picked up a piece with some blue and some white in it. She seemed uncertain about where it would go.

"It's got blue in it," Mark said, gently encouraging her.

"So it has to be sky," Connie said. "But what's the white?"

"Oh, I don't know." Mark grinned. "What's white and in the sky?"

"A cloud!" Connie said.

"Right," said Mark. "And it's got a straight edge."

"So it has to go . . ." Connie's eyes raced over the puzzle. "Here!"

"You got it," Mark said.

Connie was beaming again. Instead of picking up another piece, she turned and looked at him.

"You're nice," she said.

"Well, so are you," said Mark.

For a moment she just stared innocently at him. Then she spoke his name: "Mark?"

"Yeah?"

"Do you like living in our house?"

"Sure."

"We're gonna look after you real good," Connie said. "So you won't be sad."

She caught Mark by surprise. He wasn't sad—at least not this morning.

A door slammed somewhere in the house, and a moment later Henry stood in the doorway to the living room. He was wearing a green backpack and carrying a smaller one in his hand.

"Mark," he said. "It's oh ten hundred hours. Time to move out."

Mark glanced at Connie, who pouted.

"We'll finish the puzzle later," he said. Then he got up and headed toward Henry. Henry turned and started down the hall. He pushed the door open and held it for Mark, who stopped in the hall to get the jacket Susan had lent him. For a moment, Henry stared at him blankly as he pulled the jacket on. Then he went out onto the porch. As Mark followed him onto the porch, Henry handed him the smaller backpack. Mark heard a sound and saw Connie behind him. But as she stepped through the doorway, Henry put a hand on her chest and stopped her.

"Not you," he said.

"Why not?" Connie asked. "I'm his friend too."

"It's a military secret," Henry said.

Connie's eyes met Mark's, and he felt bad for her. He didn't mind playing with her when Henry wasn't around. But when Henry was around, it was no contest, really.

"Don't worry, Connie," Mark said. "I'll come back later and play. I promise."

Now Henry raced past him and down the steps. Mark pulled the second backpack on. There was something hard and heavy inside. He started to follow. Connie came out on the porch with tears running down her face.

"I don't care about your stupid secrets!" she shouted angrily. "I got my own secrets, and I'm not gonna tell you a single one!"

Mark paused and looked at her, somewhat shocked by the fury bursting forth from the little girl who only a minute before and been so playful and sweet.

"Hey, come on!" Henry had stopped and was waving at him.

Mark glanced one last time at Connie, then turned and hurried into the woods.

"Stay low!" Henry hissed as they ran through the woods, ducking behind trees to avoid the gunfire from an imaginary enemy. They scrambled up a wooded incline and ran down the other side through heavy brush.

"Destination: two hundred yards and closing," Henry whispered.

Mark followed him until they came to a wide pond. Several hundred yards away was the footbridge they'd raced across the day the dog had chased them. Henry stopped and crouched behind a large rock.

"Destination achieved," he said, slipping off his backpack. "Dig in."

He and Mark opened their backpacks. Inside were parts of the catapult contraption Henry had invented, as well as the rachet and some railroad spikes.

"The spike gun," Henry said, changing his voice to imitate that of a television announcer's. "Some assembly required."

Mark smiled as his cousin began to reassemble the gun. Henry could be pretty funny when he felt like it.

"So what were you and Connie doing?" Henry asked as he worked.

"Just putting together a puzzle," Mark said.

"One of those baby puzzles?" Henry asked. "You like that kind of stuff?"

"No, but she wanted me to help," Mark answered.

"You don't have to be nice to her, you know," Henry said.

"Well, I wanted to," Mark replied.

Henry didn't continue the conversation, but it was obvious to Mark that Henry didn't want him playing with his sister.

By now the spike gun was almost complete.

"Status," Henry said, getting back into the military jargon.

Mark slid a railroad spike into the slot. "System armed and ready."

"Excellent." Henry picked up the spike gun and set it on the rock. Then he began to work the ratchet back and forth. "Increasing torque. Be on the lookout for incoming."

Mark scanned the blue sky punctuated here and there by a puff of white cloud.

"Torque at maximum," Henry announced. He crouched down behind the spike gun and looked down its sight. "Scanning."

"Try to hit that rock," Mark said, pointing at a rock in the middle of the stream.

"Negative," Henry replied and kept scanning.

Mark wondered what he was looking for. He didn't have to wonder for long.

"Targeted," Henry said.

Mark looked up over the rock. On the other side of the stream was the brown and white dog—the one that had chased them over the footbridge. It was trotting along the water's edge, unaware of Henry and Mark. Henry began to move the spike gun in time with the dog. It seemed to Mark that he was aiming right at it.

"What're you doing?" Mark asked.

There was a *click* and a loud *sprong!* as the spike gun fired. Across the stream the dog was suddenly thrown sideways. It yelped loudly but then struggled back to its feet and kept walking. For a second Mark felt relieved. Henry hadn't been aiming at it after all. But then a small crimson spot appeared on the dog's side.

Mark caught his breath.

The spot started to grow larger. The dog faltered but tried to keep walking.

"Oh, my God!" Mark gasped.

By now the red spot covered the dog's entire side. His legs buckled and folded beneath him. He struggled up, almost succeeding in getting back to his feet, then finally toppled down in a heap.

One leg rose and fell. Then the dog was still.

Mark turned and stared at Henry in disbelief. Henry was still watching the dog. The expression on his face was one of wonder and awe.

"You killed it," Mark said.

Henry turned to him slowly, as if in a daze. His eyes gradually focused on Mark. For a moment Mark wondered if he'd even heard him. Then Henry spread his hands innocently and said, "I only wanted to scare it."

Mark glanced at the dog, then back at Henry. He didn't know whether to believe him or not.

"Did you see how it happened?" Henry asked. "I mean, how it just kept walking like nothing was wrong, and then it just got slower and slower until it couldn't walk anymore. I wonder what it felt like. I wonder when it knew that it was hurt."

Mark didn't share Henry's interest or fascination. He couldn't believe they'd just killed a living creature. The dog might have chased them the other day, but it was still someone's pet.

"Are you sure you didn't mean to hit it?" Mark asked.

Henry looked back at him blankly. "What do *you* think?"

"I don't know what to think," Mark said. "I mean, don't you feel bad about it?"

Henry looked back at the dog, lying unmoving beside the stream.

"You think he would have felt bad if he'd gotten us that day?" he asked.

"But he was just a dog," Mark said. "He didn't know any better."

"Now he does," Henry replied with an off-handed shrug.

Mark stared back at him in disbelief. He was almost certain now that Henry didn't care at all about what he'd done. And he would never be completely sure that his cousin hadn't intentionally fired at the dog.

"I think we better tell someone," Mark said.

Henry shook his head. "You can't."

"Why not?"

"Because we'll get into really bad trouble," Henry said. "No one will believe it was an accident. You want my parents to have to call your father in Japan and tell him you killed a dog?"

Mark was completely floored. What was Henry talking about? "I . . . I didn't kill it."

"You didn't help carry the spike gun here?" Henry asked. "You didn't help me put it together? You were the one who put the spike in it."

"But I didn't know you were going to aim it at that dog," Mark said.

"I didn't," Henry said. "It was an accident, remember?"

Mark didn't know what to say or think. It was true that he'd helped Henry, but he didn't know what the outcome would be. He'd thought they were just playing a game. He certainly didn't want to be blamed for killing the dog. And he didn't want to have to get into a situation where he had to tell his father or Wallace and Susan that it was Henry's fault, not his.

"We have to get rid of it," Henry said.

Mark looked at him in horror. "What?"

"I said, we have to get rid of it," Henry said. "We can't just leave it there and let the owner find it. Dogs run off all the time. Whoever owns it will just think it ran away."

"How are you going to get rid of it?" Mark asked.

"Not me," Henry said. "Us. We'll have to dump it down the well."

"In the cemetery?" Mark asked.

Henry nodded. Then he bent down and began to dismantle the spike gun.

"What are you doing?" Mark asked.

"I'm taking the gun apart," Henry said. "Then we'll get the dog."

It was like a bad dream. A nightmare. Mark watched Henry disassemble the gun and put it back into the packs. Henry handed the smaller pack to Mark and he put it on.

What choice did he have? Henry was his cousin and friend. They'd made a mistake, but like Henry had said, no one would believe that.

When they both had their packs on, they walked along the pond to the footbridge and crossed it. Then they began walking down the other side of the pond toward the dog.

The thought of what lay ahead repulsed Mark. "Maybe we really should tell someone," he said, slowing down.

"If you do it'll look really bad, Mark," Henry said.

"I know, but . . ."

"Look, it was an old dog anyway," Henry said. "You saw how gray its snout was. Besides, a lot of other things could have happened to it. It could have fallen off a cliff, or been run over by a car. And do you have any idea how many dogs around here get shot once hunting season begins? It happens all the time."

None of those things made Mark feel any better. Before he knew it, they were standing over the dog. At the center of the red spot, the head of the spike protruded from the dog's body. Blood dripped from its fur and ran in tiny rivulets into the pond. The dog's eyes were open and glassy, staring blankly away. Its mouth was open, and its tongue hung limp on the ground.

Without a word, Henry bent down and grabbed the dog's front legs. Then he looked up at Mark and nodded.

Feeling totally repulsed and ill, Mark bent down and slid his hands around the dog's rear legs. They still felt warm.

Henry lifted and Mark did the same. The dog's head flopped back. They started to carry the carcass back toward the footbridge.

The trip to the cemetery was horrible. Mark couldn't look at the dead creature they were carrying.

He felt terrible and guilty and ashamed. Once, when he lost his grip and the poor animal fell to the ground, Mark almost burst into tears.

Finally they arrived at the cemetery. Henry pulled the wooden cover off the well and they heaved the carcass inside. It disappeared into the darkness. Henry bent over the well wall and peered down.

There was a splash.

Henry straightened up and brought an imaginary bugle to his lips. *"Too ta too . . . Too ta toooo!"* He pretended to blow "Taps."

Mark shook his head in disgust and walked away. Sometimes Henry was funny; sometimes he wasn't.

"Hey, where's your sense of humor?" Henry called after him.

Mark didn't reply. He was starting to think his cousin was really sick.

12

"Is something wrong?"

Mark blinked and looked up into Susan's face. He was at the kitchen table with Henry. It was lunchtime.

"You haven't touched your sandwich," Susan said.

Mark stared down at the bacon, lettuce, and tomato sandwich on toast that lay on his plate. Across the table from him, Henry had finished his sandwich and was munching on some carrot sticks.

"Well, I guess I'm just not hungry," Mark said.

"Are you feeling all right?" Susan asked.

Mark nodded, although he couldn't get the memory of that morning out of his head.

"It's very unusual for a boy your age not to have any appetite," Susan said.

Mark looked across at Henry.

"We had some cookies in town this morning," Henry said.

"Ah ha." Susan nodded. "That explains it."

Mark was really tempted to tell her that wasn't the reason at all. Then Henry caught his eye. He didn't move a muscle; he just stared. *Don't blow it,* his eyes seemed to say. Mark looked down at his sandwich and took a bite.

After lunch Henry said he had to go outside and take care of something. Mark didn't ask him what it was. He'd had enough of Henry's projects for the time being.

Henry went off, and Mark left the kitchen and wandered into the living room again. Connie's puzzle lay unfinished on the coffee table. It looked as if she'd never gone back to it after he'd left with Henry that morning.

Mark wondered where Connie was. She hadn't been home for lunch, so she must be at a friend's house playing. He missed her, in a way. She was sweet and innocent, and he didn't have to worry about her doing strange things.

Suddenly Mark had nothing to do. He glanced out the window and saw that the sky had become gray with clouds. It didn't look very inviting outside; and besides, Henry was out there and Mark didn't want to see him.

There was a big piano in the living room with a bunch of framed photographs on the top. Mark wandered over to it and struck a key with his finger. A note rang out, but it didn't sound right.

Mark began to look at the pictures. A lot of them were of Wallace, Susan, Henry, and Connie. Some were summer shots of them in light clothes, others were taken in the middle of a snowy winter. There were other photographs of them with people Mark didn't know—obviously friends or other relatives.

Then a small black and white photo in a silver frame caught his eye. It was his mother, holding a small child. His mother was wearing a dress. Her hair was long, and she looked very healthy. Mark turned the frame over. On the back someone had written "Janice and Mark, 1983."

Mark felt tears rise uncontrollably into his eyes.

It was all so hard to believe.

It was all so unfair.

It made him feel so bad.

He turned the frame over again and looked down at the photograph. A tear splashed against the glass. Then another.

"Mark?"

Startled, Mark spun around, accidentally knocking several of the photographs off the piano with his arm. They fell to the rug with a muffled crash.

"Oh, gosh, I'm sorry," Mark gasped, quickly rubbing the tears out of his eyes and kneeling down. "I didn't mean to . . ."

"It's all right," Susan said, joining him.

"I'm really sorry," Mark said. He started picking up the pictures. So far none of them appeared to be broken.

"It's no big deal," Susan said.

"I swear it was an accident," Mark blurted. "Really."

Susan looked at him with a funny smile. "I believe you, Mark. And anyway, nothing's broken. We'll just put them all back the way they were and everything will be . . ."

Her words trailed off as she caught sight of the photograph that Mark still held in his hand. "Oh, Mark," she said, softly and sadly.

Mark gazed down, unable to look her in the eye.

"Maybe I should have put that picture away," Susan said.

"No, it's okay," Mark said. He looked down at the photograph. "Did you like my mom?"

"Oh, yes," Susan replied. "Everybody did."

"That's what everybody says. You're not just saying that, are you?"

"No. She was a wonderful person. And she loved you very much."

Mark squeezed the frame in his hand. "The last time I saw her . . . she said she'd always be with me."

"It's true," Susan said. "People die, but they stay with you. They never leave you."

As Susan said this, she bent down and picked up one last photograph. It was of a boy, maybe two years old, wearing light blue pajamas and holding a toy rubber whale. Susan grew quiet.

"Is that Richard?" Mark asked.

Susan nodded. Her eyes met Mark's.

"Your mother is alive in you," she said. "She'll always be a part of you."

"And Richard in you?" Mark asked.

"Yes."

Mark gazed up into her warm brown eyes and felt it again. It was a special feeling he had only with Susan. It was as though they shared a secret knowledge no one else knew. As if in some strange, sad way, even though she was a lot older, they were best friends.

Suddenly Mark felt someone else in the room. He turned and saw Henry standing in the doorway. He didn't know why, but he had a feeling his cousin had been standing there and watching for a while. Now Susan turned and saw him.

"Oh, hi, Henry," she said.

"Hi." Henry's tone was flat and empty. It was very different from the animated and energetic boy Mark knew. Now he turned toward Mark. "Come on. I want to show you something in the garage."

Mark turned back and gave Susan a questioning look.

"Go on," she said, placing her hand on his shoulder and giving him a gentle push.

Mark took a few steps and then stopped.

"What's in the garage?" he heard Susan ask behind him.

"It's a surprise," Henry said.

"You and your surprises," Susan said. But there was no anger in her voice. Instead, she sounded amused and fond of her secretive son.

Mark stood in the middle of the room. He didn't want to go.

"You coming?" Henry asked.

Mark glanced back at Susan. He didn't want to say anything about what had happened that morning in front of her.

"Hey, come on," Henry said.

Again Mark glanced at Susan, almost pleading with his eyes.

"Go ahead," Susan said. "You don't have to stay for my sake."

If only she knew, Mark thought. He followed Henry reluctantly. Outside, the air felt colder than it had that morning. The sky was like a huge slab of slate, and the air felt damp. Mark walked very slowly. He wasn't certain he wanted to know what the next surprise was. As they crossed the lawn toward the garage, Henry suddenly turned and looked back at him.

"Look, I'm really sorry about the dog," he said earnestly. "But it really was an accident. You don't think I'd really do something like that on purpose, do you?"

Mark didn't know what to think.

Henry stopped and pointed back at the house. "Look," he said, "if you really want me to, I'll go back inside and tell my mom what happened. I mean, I know it'll get us in a lot of trouble we don't deserve. But if it'll really make you feel better . . ."

Mark sighed. Somehow he'd managed to survive for several hours since that awful incident. Nothing terrible had happened to him. Lightning hadn't struck. The dog was gone. Nothing they could say or do would bring it back.

"Let's forget about it," Mark said. Despite feeling wary, he was glad in a way to be relieved of the boredom he'd felt when he had no one to fool around with. "So, what did you want to show me?"

Henry smiled. "I want you to meet somebody. Somebody really special. He's in here."

They reached the garage and Henry started to open the side door. Mark reached for his arm and stopped. Henry turned, surprised.

"What?"

"Can I trust you?" Mark asked.

His cousin stared back at him. He knew what Mark meant: He didn't want any more trouble.

Henry smiled. "Hey, we're blood brothers."

Mark watched him slip into the dark garage. It was strange how Henry affected him. Half the time he was worried what the kid would do next. The other half the time he couldn't wait to find out.

Mark stepped into the garage just as Henry flicked on the fluorescent lights. Mark caught his breath. A man wearing a wrinkled suit was sitting in a chair in the shadows, facing away from them. He was wearing a navy-blue wool cap, and his head was tilted forward as if he was asleep.

"Who . . ." Mark started to ask.

Henry quickly pressed a finger to his lips. "Shhh. It's Mr. Highway."

"But who is he?" Mark whispered back.

Henry tiptoed toward him, reached forward, and tilted Mr. Highway's head back. The head flopped back, and Mark immediately saw that Mr. Highway had no face. Instead, there was a small old lampshade with the cap pulled over it.

Mr. Highway was a dummy.

"He's a suicide," Henry whispered.

"What're you talking about?" Mark asked.

"He wants to die," Henry said.

Henry was talking nonsense. Mark reached for the head and tilted it back. Inside, the suit was filled with old batting from a mattress or something.

"You made him?" Mark asked.

Henry nodded.

"What are you going to do with him?"

Henry stepped away from the dummy and toward Mark. "That depends."

"On what?"

"On you," Henry said.

It was another challenge. Mark could feel it. He'd promised himself he wouldn't take any more challenges from Henry, and yet he could feel himself getting sucked in. *What did his cousin have planned this time?*

"Why me?" Mark asked.

"Will you help me?" asked Henry.

"Do what?"

Henry's eyes sparkled. Mark recognized the look. It was the way Henry always looked when he had a plan.

"I promise you'll see something you'll never forget," Henry said.

"Does it involve any animals?" Mark asked.

Henry laughed out loud. "No."

"Standing on the edge of any cliffs?" asked Mark.

Henry shook his head. "So, are you in or out?"

The alternative was hanging around the house with nothing to do. Besides, it wouldn't hurt to just *see* what Henry had in mind. But this time he'd be on his guard. At the slightest hint of trouble, he'd back out.

"In."

The word was hardly out of Mark's mouth before Henry turned away and reached under his worktable. He pulled out an old moth-eaten blanket.

"Help me spread it," he said.

Mark grabbed one end and helped spread the blanket on the floor. He didn't even bother to ask what Henry had planned, since he knew the only answer he'd receive would be "You'll see."

"Okay, let's get Mr. Highway," Henry said once the blanket was on the floor.

Together they took Mr. Highway by the arms and laid him in the blanket.

"Let's roll it up," Henry said. Together they rolled up the blanket with Mr. Highway inside.

When that was done, Henry went to one end of the blanket. "I'll get this end and you get that end."

Mark couldn't resist any longer. He was overcome with curiosity. "What are we doing?" he asked. "And don't say, you'll see."

"All right," Henry said as they headed out the door, each of them carrying one end of the blanket. "We are going to help Mr. Highway."

Outside, a few flakes of snow had started to drift down out of the gray sky. Henry reached the road and turned to walk alongside it. Mark followed, holding up his end. He was distracted by the sight of the small white flakes floating out of the sky and landing on his head and jacket. Snow! Real, live snow! Of course, he'd seen the stuff on TV a bunch of times, but this was the first time he'd actually experienced it for real. Flakes landed on his nose, tickling him. They got caught in his eyelashes. It was weird how they just landed on the cold ground and stayed there.

Ahead, carrying the front end of the blanket, Henry marched on, oblivious to the miraculous white stuff floating out of the sky. Mark started to feel funny again. Maybe this was a mistake. Maybe he shouldn't have agreed so easily. Now here he was involved in another of Henry's schemes. Already he felt sort of trapped. If he changed his mind now, he'd be leaving Henry with Mr. Highway wrapped in the blanket— too awkward a bundle for one kid to handle alone.

The snowflakes were starting to collect on the road, where they were blown around by small gusts of wind. There were still too few to mean anything, but it made Mark wonder. He didn't want to go too far and get stuck in a snowstorm or anything.

"Where are we going?" he asked.

"Not far," Henry replied.

The road curved ahead, and as they approached the curve, Mark began to hear a familiar sound. At first he couldn't place it there in the middle of rural Maine. But as they got closer, the sound grew louder, and Mark realized what it was.

The sound of cars on a highway.

They entered the curve. Ahead, Mark could see that the road they were walking along crossed over a six-lane highway. Mark was surprised at the number of cars that whizzed by, even out there in rural Maine.

"Where are all these cars going?" he asked.

"I don't know," Henry replied. "Bangor, Portland, places like that."

They kept walking until they came to the bridge. It was made of concrete and steel. On either side of the roadway—separated by a low concrete barrier from the cars—was a pedestrian walkway. Beside the walkway was a green metal rail to prevent anyone from falling onto the highway below.

Now what? Mark wondered.

After pausing for a moment, Henry continued onto

the bridge with Mark following, holding the other end of the blanket. As cars raced by below, Mark could see the occupants looking up at them through their windshields for an instant before disappearing beneath the bridge.

"Let's put him down," Henry said.

Together they lowered the blanket to the walkway. As Mark watched, Henry started to unwrap Mr. Highway.

"What are you gonna do?" Mark asked.

"Mr. Highway needs some air," Henry said.

Moments later Henry had the dummy unwrapped and he picked him up, leaning him against the railing.

"Come on, Mr. Highway," he said. "Take a look."

Mark and Henry stood on either side of the dummy, staring down at the busy roadway. They were standing right over the fast lane. Mark imagined that to the motorists passing below they looked like two boys standing with an old man.

"Life's been hard for Mr. Highway," Henry said. "His wife divorced him and his kids ran away. His house burned down and his car was stolen."

Mark couldn't help smiling. It was all sad stuff, but this was pretend, and Henry made it sound funny. Henry said something more, but a big truck roared under the bridge at that moment and drowned him out.

"What did you say?" Mark asked.

"I said, poor old Mr. Highway's thinking about the end," Henry said.

"Oh yeah?"

"Yeah. He's had enough of this terrible life," Henry said. He said something more, but again a truck drowned him out.

"What?" Mark shouted over the roar.

"Say goodbye!" Henry yelled back.

The next thing Mark knew, Henry picked up the dummy. In a flash, Mark had a horrible realization.

"Don't!" he cried.

Too late. Henry heaved Mr. Highway over the railing.

13

EVERYTHING SEEMED TO HAPPEN IN SLOW MOTION. MARK pressed himself against the cold metal railing and watched as Mr. Highway tumbled down below. He could see the horrified looks on the faces of the drivers in the cars racing toward them.

It must have looked like a man had just jumped.

Screeeeech! In the fast lane, a car's brakes locked and it skidded sideways as it approached the bridge and the figure of a man falling toward the ground.

Clank! The skidding car banged into a car in the middle lane. Both cars stayed side by side, locked in a weird, violent, skidding dance. A third car behind them braked hard, fishtailed, and began to spin.

Meanwhile the two cars locked together veered into the slow lane.

Mark watched in frozen terror. Someone was going to be killed. People were going to be maimed.

And all because of him.

Out of the corner of his eye he could see Henry, his arms raised triumphantly and an exultant expression on his face. He was shouting something, but Mark couldn't hear it over the skidding cars and blaring horns.

Crunch! A car in the slow lane piled into the rear end of the other two, scattering them across the roadway.

And then it was over. Three dented, mangled cars lay at odd angles on the highway. For a moment everything was still. The only sounds were a stuck horn blaring and steam hissing out of a sprung hood.

Then there was a creaking sound as someone inside one of the cars pushed a battered door open. Mark watched from above, transfixed. Now another sound reached his ears: the sound of children wailing in fear.

It was coming from one of the damaged cars. A station wagon with fake wood paneling.

Was a child hurt?

Or dead?

Mark felt a terrible chill and the horrendous feeling of remorse. What an awful thing! How could he have taken part in it? He never would have done anything like this. *Never!* If he'd even suspected what Henry had planned, he would have refused instantly. But he'd never even suspected. It was such an outrageous, terrible thing to do. Something he'd never even *imagined*.

Tears began to fill his eyes. Then he felt someone tugging at his jacket. It had to be Henry, but Mark couldn't look at him.

The battered car door finally opened and a man squeezed out. He hurried across the highway to the station wagon. Mark watched as the man grabbed the station wagon's door and yanked it open. A woman staggered out.

"Are you okay?" the man shouted.

"Yes, yes, I think so."

The man looked over her shoulder into the back of the station wagon. "Those kids?"

"They're okay," the woman gasped. "We're all okay."

Other people approached the accident scene. They were running from other cars. Wiping the tears out of his eyes, Mark looked up and saw that cars had stopped in all three lanes and were starting to back up. Those people in the cars closest to the accident had gotten out. Some stood and watched, while others ran toward the battered cars to see if they could help.

"Come on," Mark heard Henry say as he tugged on his sleeve again. Mark didn't move. It was awful, terrible, the worst thing . . .

The people in the third car got out. It seemed amazing and even miraculous to Mark that no one appeared to be injured. Now the man who'd pulled open the station-wagon door turned away from the woman with the children and started toward the fast lane.

Toward Mr. Highway.

"Come on," Henry hissed, and he yanked hard on Mark's jacket. "We gotta go!"

Yes, they had to run or they'd get caught. More to the point, Mark knew *he'd* get caught.

For being part of something he never would have agreed to.

If only he'd known.

The next thing he knew, he and Henry were racing off the bridge and back down the road. Mark looked behind and just caught a glimpse of the man leaning over Mr. Highway. Then the man frowned and looked up at the bridge where only a few seconds before Mark and Henry had been standing.

"Incredible!" As they ran, Henry leaped into the air and raised his fists.

New tears flooded into Mark's eyes. He didn't understand why Henry would want to do such a thing, but it made him feel awful. He realized that Henry was looking at him as they ran.

"Did you see that?" His cousin gasped with excited delight. "It was fantastic! Twenty, thirty cars! We did it! We did it!"

We? Mark was filled with a miserable mix of remorse and dread. How had it happened? How could he have been part of it?

Suddenly Mark felt a hand grab his arm and pull him to a stop. Henry stood beside him stock-still, listening. At first Mark didn't hear anything. All he was aware of was the snow, which had started to fall more heavily around them.

Then he heard it: the faint sound of a siren.

More than one. Lots of them. All growing louder. Now Mark could see blue and red flashing lights in the distance through the trees. A whole procession of flashing blue and red lights and wailing sirens growing louder. Mark felt Henry's grip on his arm grow tighter.

"Down here!" Henry gasped, pulling him down from the road into a ditch.

Their feet slid on the grassy, snowy embankment. Mark hit the bottom of the ditch and stood as if in a daze.

"Come on!" Henry hissed, the exuberance in his voice now replaced by a tone of annoyance. Once again he grabbed Mark's arm and began to pull him, this time along the ditch.

"What are you doing?" Mark asked. "Where are we—"

"Just be quiet," Henry snapped.

The blaring sirens were growing louder. Mark could hear the sounds of whining engines as well.

Ahead of them, a large concrete culvert ran under the road. It was a big empty pipe that allowed water to run under the road during the wet season.

"In here," Henry said, pulling Mark down and into the pipe. They both crouched down with their backs resting against the curving walls of the culvert. Once again, Mark was overcome with bewilderment and regret.

"I didn't know," he stammered. "I just didn't know. . . . I couldn't . . . I don't understand why you did it. . . ."

"Just shut up," Henry hissed.

Moments later the ground above them thundered as the police cars and emergency vehicles raced overhead. Mark crouched in miserable stunned silence.

It was the worst nightmare. He couldn't believe what Henry had done. The kid was crazy. Anyone who could do such a thing had to be.

The last police car roared overhead, and it began to grow quiet again. Mark felt a hand fall lightly on his shoulder. His head jerked up and he found himself staring into Henry's eyes.

The confident, charming smile.

The eerie calm within, despite what he'd just done.

Mark stared at him, incredulous.

"Hey, relax," Henry said. "Nobody got hurt."

"That's not the point," Mark replied.

"Wait a minute. I didn't know those drivers were going to act like that," Henry said, suddenly filled with innocence. "I mean, they just freaked out."

Mark couldn't stand any more of his bull. "Do you know what you did?"

The smile on Henry's face surprised him. "What *I* did? Hey, come on. *We* did it together!"

"You could've killed people," Mark said.

"With *your* help."

Mark shook his head angrily. "No way. I didn't know you were going to do that."

Henry just gazed back at him, his expression somewhere between a smile and a smirk. "Oh, really? I think you were kind of encouraging me all the way, Mark. I mean, I didn't do this kind of thing until you came along."

Mark stared at him in disbelief. Had he heard Henry correctly? Was the kid actually blaming *him?* Mark was so taken aback by the idea that he couldn't get the words out of his mouth to deny it. Henry slid closer.

"Hey, don't worry," he said in a conspiratorial tone. "I won't tell anyone as long as you don't, blood brother."

Mark just stared back at him, almost dazed by the insanity of the whole situation.

"Come on," Henry said, moving even closer. "Why don't you just admit it? You enjoyed it as much as I did."

Enjoyed it?

Henry had started to back off, but now it was Mark's turn to reach out and grab his arm. For a moment the two boys locked eyes.

"You're sick," Mark whispered.

He thought Henry might get mad or even want to fight, but his cousin just smiled.

"Listen, Mark," he said, "I promised you something amazing. Something you'd never forget. Where's the gratitude?"

Mark looked at him in disbelief. *Gratitude?* It was as if Henry thought it was some kind of joke or game. He could've killed half a dozen people. He *had* wrecked their cars and scared the life out of them.

It was as though he didn't care.

Mark pushed himself up and duckwalked back out of the culvert. He stood up in the ditch and looked through the woods toward the highway. He could just make out the flashing blue and red lights through the trees and falling snowflakes. He could hear the shouts of tow-truck operators working to hook the wrecks up and move them away. The curiosity of the other drivers had been replaced by impatience, and he could hear car horns beeping as people waited for the lanes to reopen.

So much hardship and damage and pain. And Henry thought it was just a big joke.

Without looking back into the culvert, Mark climbed up the slippery side of the ditch and back onto the shoulder of the road. He started to walk home.

"Hey." He heard Henry's voice behind him and immediately crossed to the other side of the road without looking back. He just wanted to get away from him.

Henry crossed the road behind him. "Aw, Mr. Righteous-Goody-Two-Shoes."

Mark quickly crossed back to the other side of the road. This time Henry didn't follow.

14

HE WAS QUIET DURING DINNER AND BARELY TOUCHED HIS food. His stomach felt as though it was in a knot: a knot of guilt over what had happened, confusion over what to do about it, and fear of what would happen next. Susan asked if something was wrong and Mark almost told her, but somehow he couldn't bring himself to say it. At least not to *her*. So instead he made up a little story about eating some candy before dinner that must have ruined his appetite.

All through dinner Henry seemed to stare at him. But it wasn't as if he was worried or scared that Mark might say something. Every time Mark glanced in his direction, Henry looked back with an almost bemused expression on his face. Almost as if he was *daring* Mark to say something.

After dinner, Mark went into the kitchen and helped with the dishes. Susan was standing at the sink wearing an apron and yellow rubber gloves. She was rinsing the dishes and putting them into the dishwasher. Mark joined her, scraping the leftovers off the plates and into the disposal.

"Oh, Mark," Susan said, "you don't have to help."

"I want to," Mark said.

"Why don't you go play with Henry?"

Mark shrugged. Susan glanced at him and frowned. "It seems like something's bothering you. Is it because your father's only called once since he went away?"

That wasn't the reason. His father had called after he'd landed in Tokyo. He'd warned Mark that it might be difficult to call for the next few days. He was going to be very busy, and the time difference was such that he'd be able to call only when Mark was asleep.

No, that wasn't the reason. But Mark couldn't tell Susan the real reason he was so gloomy, so he'd use his father as an excuse.

"Sort of," Mark said.

Susan nodded sympathetically. "It must be difficult for you right now."

Mark nodded back. It was strange how his other problems had receded in the face of this new problem, namely Henry. Mark was really tempted to tell her about it. But how could he? Even though he felt a strong bond with Susan, he hardly knew her. And she hardly knew him. Why would she ever believe him?

"When did he say he'd call again?" Susan asked.

"When he had the time," Mark said. "I understand that it's hard for him. He's got to do a lot while he's there."

Susan nodded and smiled slightly. "It's good that you understand that, Mark. A lot of boys your age wouldn't."

Even after the dishes were done, he sat at the kitchen table pretending to read some old Sunday comics, but really just trying to avoid Henry and the whole issue of what had happened that day.

Susan and Connie sat at a window seat near the kitchen window. Connie was cuddled in her mother's arms, and together they watched the snowflakes float down through the lights outside.

Susan had a small color TV in the kitchen, and she usually listened to the local evening news while she cleaned. Mark wasn't paying attention until he heard something about a four-car accident closing down all the lanes of a highway.

Mark looked up and felt the blood drain from his face. There on the TV was the same view from the bridge he'd had earlier that afternoon. First the scattered wrecks intermingled with police cars, emergency vehicles, and tow trucks. Then three long lines of cars backed up and waiting for the highway to reopen.

The TV crew must have shot it from up on the bridge.

Now the scene on the TV switched from day to night, and a woman with red hair stepped in front of the camera. She was holding a microphone and trying to brush the falling snow off her shoulders as she talked. In the background, headlights flashed past and disappeared under the bridge.

"And that was the way it was for several hours this afternoon," she was saying. "As you can see now, things are moving again. But traffic was backed up for three miles on the northbound side. Even after the cars blocking the route were cleared, traffic continued to move slowly for several hours while police and tow-truck operators cleared debris from the road."

The scene now jumped back to the studio, and the woman on the bridge became a face on a newsroom monitor. A gray-haired man sitting at a news desk was turned toward the monitor.

"Now you say, Monica, that no one was hurt," the gray-haired man said.

"That's right, Jim," said the red-haired woman.

"Ambulances had been sent to the scene, but they weren't needed. Several local law-enforcement officials have told me that it was a miracle no one was injured."

Mark felt the knot in his stomach grow tighter. He couldn't stand it. He had to talk to someone, had to get it off his chest and out of his stomach. And he had to do it *now!*

Filled with determination, Mark stood up so abruptly that he accidentally knocked over the chair he'd been sitting in. It fell over with a crash.

Susan turned from the sink and gave him a puzzled look as he quickly righted the chair. "Are you all right, Mark?"

For a second Mark just stared back at her. It was on the tip of his tongue. . . .

"Is something wrong?" Susan asked.

"No." He couldn't tell her. Not *her.*

He walked out of the kitchen and down the hall to Wallace's study. Henry's father had said something about doing a little work after dinner. Now, through the half-open study door, Mark could see Wallace's back as he sat at his desk.

Mark walked slowly down the hall toward him. He was trying to collect his thoughts. Wallace was the person he had to tell. Wallace was . . . *in charge.* He was the father, the boss. He'd know what to do.

As Mark stepped down the hall, he passed an open doorway to his right. Inside it was dark. Suddenly, a whisper sprang out: "Go ahead. Tell him."

Mark jumped. His heart began to race. A moment later Henry appeared out of the dark. Henry moved closer, a half-smile on his lips—the same expression he'd had all through dinner. Mark felt his throat grow tight.

"Better yet," Mark's cousin whispered, "why don't we tell him together?"

"Drop dead," Mark whispered back, glancing nervously down the hall. Through the doorway he could see that Wallace was still hunched over his desk, unaware of the conversation taking place out in the hallway behind him.

"It was Mark, Dad," Henry whispered in an innocent tone, pretending to be speaking to his father. "He talked me into doing it. I thought he was just playing a game. I had no idea what he was going to do."

Mark stared back at him in stunned silence. Those were almost exactly the words he had planned to use. Suddenly he could picture it: Both of them standing there, insisting it was the other's idea. Who would Wallace believe? Maybe Henry. Maybe neither of them. But one thing was for certain: Henry's father wasn't about to choose Mark's word over that of his own son.

"Please, Dad, go easy on him," Henry continued in his mocking whisper. "He can't help it if he's all screwed up because he misses his mommy. . . ."

Mark tried to push him away, but Henry grabbed his arm and started to pull him down the hall toward the study.

"What are you stalling for?" Henry hissed. "Let's go."

But Mark pulled back. He didn't want to talk to Wallace anymore. He just wanted to get away from this crazy kid.

"Dad!" Henry called down the hall. "Mark's got something he wants to tell you."

"Stop it!" Mark tried to push Henry away.

But his cousin held on. He was completely crazy. Out of his mind. Mark broke free and started back down the hall. Behind him the hall filled with light as Wallace turned around and opened the study door. Mark took the steps two at a time but then stopped and listened.

"What's going on?" he heard Wallace ask Henry. "What's wrong with Mark?"

"I don't know," he heard Henry reply. "He's been acting pretty weird lately. I better go see if he's okay."

Mark turned and started climbing up the steps again. He didn't know what he was going to do, only that he had to do something.

It wasn't a game anymore. Henry was acting crazy. Even worse, he was acting as though he wanted to get Mark.

He reached the top of the stairs. Now what? The only choice seemed to be Henry's room. Mark went in and closed the door behind him. He turned on the light. He had to think, had to figure out a way to deal with this. He sat down on the bed with his back to the door.

A few seconds later he heard footsteps in the hall. Then a creak as the door opened.

"There you are," Henry said.

Mark stiffened involuntarily. Henry really gave him the creeps.

More footsteps. Then the squeaking of bedsprings as Henry flopped down on his bed. Mark turned slightly and glanced out of the corner of his eye. Henry was lying on his back with his hands clasped behind his head, smiling victoriously. "I told Dad I'd see if you were okay. Are you okay, Mark?"

The words were filled with menace and laughter, as if Henry knew he'd won.

This round.

"Leave me alone," Mark muttered.

"Leave you alone?" Henry asked with an amused tone. "This is *my* room."

Ignore him, Mark told himself. Don't pay any attention. Don't have anything to do with him. Just wait until Dad comes back and then get out of this crazy place forever.

Now there was another set of footsteps. Lighter ones.

"Guess what?" It was Connie's voice. Mark turned around. Henry's little sister was standing in the doorway.

"What?" Henry asked tersely.

Connie stepped into the room. "Mom says I can stay up late tonight."

"Connie, what are you doing?" Henry asked, getting up from the bed.

"What?" Connie asked.

Henry walked toward her, glowering. "What did I tell you about coming into my room?"

"But you're not working on anything," Connie said.

Henry cupped his right hand like a crab's pincers and closed it around the back of his sister's neck.

"Ow!" Connie yelped. "That hurts. Let go."

Henry held tight while his sister squirmed in pain.

"Please, Henry," she cried. "You're hurting me!"

"You didn't answer my question," Henry said.

"Ow!" Connie cried. "I forget."

"Okay," Henry said, "I'll answer it for you: You are not allowed in here. Not now. Not ever. Never!"

Mark had been watching from the bed, but now he got up. He couldn't stand the way Henry bullied his sister. It wasn't normal. It was weird and sick.

Just like Henry.

Connie was much smaller than him, and yet he didn't care at all how much pain he caused her. Well, Mark had had enough of Henry's meanness.

"Did you hear—" Henry wasn't able to finish the sentence, because Mark grabbed him by the throat and yanked him away from Connie, cutting off his words and forcing him back toward the beds.

"Urggh . . ." A gurgling sound came from Henry as he tried to pry Mark's hands off his neck. Mark forced him across the room and slammed him as hard as he could against the wall. He glared into Henry's surprised eyes.

"You're wrong," Mark said, barely able to contain his fury. "This is my room too. And I say she can stay."

The surprised look vanished from Henry's eyes and was replaced by an angry squint. But at the same time, a strange smile appeared on his lips. It was the look of a challenge accepted. Henry slowly worked his fingers in between his neck and Mark's hands. Mark wasn't trying to choke Henry, he was only trying to keep him backed against the wall and away from Connie.

Henry managed to pry Mark's hands from his neck. The two boys were locked in a fierce stare. As Mark felt his hands lose their grip, he quickly reached up and grabbed two handfuls of Henry's hair. Now Henry did the same, and Mark felt the intense pain as his cousin's hands each grabbed a tuft of hair and pulled.

The boys were locked together, their heads tilted down like rams in battle, each with a firm grip on the other's hair, neither willing to give in and acknowledge the pain.

"Mom! Mom!" Mark heard Connie shout and run out of the room.

The pain was killing Mark, but he wouldn't let go. It felt as if Henry was trying to rip the hair from his head. Unwanted tears forced their way out of his eyes, but he wouldn't give in to this nutcase who called himself his cousin. Slowly both their heads twisted, their faces red and contorted with pain and grim determination.

"So, you like my little sister." Henry's words took on an almost fiendish quality.

"Drop dead, jerk." Mark spat the words out.

"Such a sweet little girl," Henry hissed. "It would be too bad if something happened to her. If she got . . . hurt. You'd be sad, wouldn't you, Mark?"

From anyone else it would have been just an idle threat. But from Henry it could be real. Why should he stop at killing dogs and almost killing strangers?

Besides, Mark already knew that Henry couldn't stand sharing things. Why should it stop at footballs and jackets? There were no limits with his cousin. He did anything he wanted to do.

"You wouldn't dare!" Mark gasped. The thought was incredible—that Henry would really hurt his little sister.

"Hey, accidents happen," Henry whispered with a nasty chuckle. "Just ask my mom about Richard."

"You're sick," Mark whispered back.

"Henry! Mark!" Susan's voice startled them. Mark and Henry instantly let go and turned to the doorway, where Henry's mother stood, staring at them. For a moment Mark was lost in the relief of pain ended.

"What's going on, Henry?" his mother asked, stepping into the room.

Mark watched in amazement as Henry transformed himself from a vicious, menacing tormentor into the smiling, charming boy who seemed incapable of doing anyone harm. He bowed his head and stepped toward his mother, somehow projecting an innocent boyish sense of regret.

"I'm sorry, Mom," he said sheepishly. "We were playing this really dumb game."

He glanced back at Mark, as if telling him to play along.

"It didn't look like a game to me," Susan said. "It looked like you two were fighting."

"I know it must have looked that way, but we

weren't fighting," Henry said. "We were just playing. Weren't we, Mark?"

Mark could feel Susan's questioning gaze on him. He wished he could tell her the truth, but he was certain she would never believe him.

"Yeah." Mark's reply was barely more than a mumble. "We were just playing."

Henry grinned. Mark hated that grin. Across the room, Susan looked relieved.

"Well, don't play so rough," she said. "For a second there you looked like you were trying to kill each other."

She turned and left the room. Henry looked at Mark with that awful, triumphant smile on his face. As Mark glared back with a mixture of anger and fear, he remembered what Henry had said about his little sister.

"Don't you dare do anything to Connie," Mark said.

Henry just smiled and walked out of the room.

It was dark when Mark heard Henry come back into the bedroom. Mark lay in his bed and listened. The room was dark, and he could just make out Henry's dark silhouette. He watched the boy closely. Would he do anything? Try to hurt Mark in some way?

Henry stayed on his side of the room. Without a word, he changed into his pajamas and got into bed.

But that didn't mean he'd stay in bed.

What if Henry waited until the middle of the night, when he was certain Mark was asleep? What if he tried to do something then?

Mark wondered how he'd get any sleep that night. He stared up at the dark ceiling. He just didn't get it. He didn't understand how the kid could be that way. Henry had a healthy mother and a father who was around most of the time. He should *appreciate* that. He should be a happy kid, not this cruel, mean person who delighted in causing others pain and misery.

Yes, that was the thing that troubled Mark the most. Why? Why was Henry like that?

15

BRIGHT SUNLIGHT WAS STREAMING THROUGH THE CUR-
tains when Mark awoke the next morning. Immediately he glanced at Henry's bed. The bed was empty,
and a slight shiver ran through Mark. He'd stayed up
for a long time last night, but obviously he'd finally
fallen asleep. Just the thought of himself asleep,
defenseless, in the same room with Henry, unnerved
him.

Mark got up and went to the window. He had to
squint in the bright light. Outside, the sun was shin-
ing, and its light was reflected off the thick blanket of
newly fallen snow. Mark had never seen so much
snow. It covered every inch of ground, as well as every
bush and tree. For a moment, Mark forgot about all
his other concerns and worries and just wanted to go
outside and jump in the stuff. He wanted to do all the
things he'd heard of but had never been able to do,
like make snowmen and snow angels and have snow-
ball fights.

Then he glanced again at Henry's empty, unmade
bed.

No, he couldn't play today. There was something else he had to do. He just hoped he wasn't already too late.

Mark dressed quickly and hurried downstairs. He could somehow sense that Henry was not only out of his room but out of the house. It was weird how the house felt different when Henry wasn't there, as if his presence somehow darkened the atmosphere. When Henry wasn't there, the house felt warmer, lighter, and brighter.

Or maybe it was just his imagination.

Mark went into the kitchen. Susan was standing by the sink, doing the dishes. It looked as if breakfast was finished.

"Where's Connie?" Mark asked.

Susan turned from the sink and gave him a funny look. "She was here a moment ago, why?"

"She didn't go out, did she?" Mark asked.

"No, I don't think so. Is something wrong?"

"Uh . . ." Mark realized he probably should have been a bit more subtle. "No, no. I was just wondering," he said with a yawn.

Susan frowned. "You look tired."

Mark sort of shrugged.

"Hungry?" Susan asked.

Mark nodded and glanced around. "Have you seen Henry?"

"He went out about an hour ago," Susan said. "On another one of his secret missions. So, what would you like for breakfast?"

"Oh, anything you've got." Mark walked over to the doorway to the living room and looked through it, hoping he'd see Connie there. She wasn't.

"Looking for something?" Susan asked.

"Uh, not really." Mark came back to the kitchen table. If Connie was still in the house, he'd hear the door slam when she went out.

"How about scrambled eggs and toast?" Susan asked.

"Sounds great."

Mark sat down at the table, but he couldn't get comfortable. He was on edge. What if Connie *had* gone outside?

What if Henry was out there waiting for her?

If any other kid in the world had implied that he was going to do something bad to his little sister, Mark would have ignored it.

But not when Henry said it.

The kitchen door swung open and Connie came in, dressed in a pink snowsuit, white boots, and mittens.

"You got dressed all by yourself!" Susan said, delight in her voice.

Connie nodded and beamed proudly.

"Well, you're becoming my big little girl," Susan said.

"Can I go out and play in the snow?" Connie asked.

"Of course you can," Susan said. "Go right ahead."

Connie turned to leave.

"Hey, wait!" Mark said.

Connie stopped. "What?"

"How'd you like to play with me?" Mark asked.

"Uh, okay." Connie grinned shyly. "I'm going to the playground. I'll meet you there."

"No," Mark said quickly.

Connie scowled.

"What is it, Mark?" Susan asked over the sizzling sound of raw eggs hitting a hot skillet.

"Well, I was just wondering if Connie would wait for me, that's all," Mark said.

"Why can't she go ahead?" Susan asked.

"Well, uh . . ." Mark had to think fast. "I don't really know how to get to the playground."

"It's easy," Connie said. "You just go down the driveway and make a left and you'll see it."

"Well, I'd still like to walk there with you," Mark said. "I mean, I won't be too long. All I have to do is eat breakfast and throw on my boots and a warm jacket."

Susan gave him another funny look, then turned to Connie.

"Would you wait?" Susan asked.

"But I'm getting hot," Connie said.

"Maybe you could play outside until Mark is ready," her mother said.

"Okay." Connie smiled warmly at Mark. "I'll see you outside."

"Great." Mark waved at her and then glanced back at Susan, hoping the whole scene hadn't appeared too strange. Susan looked back at him. She cocked her head slightly to the side, puzzled.

"What is it, Mark?" she asked.

"Nothing, really. I just feel like I spend a lot of time with Henry, and Connie gets ignored a lot. I thought she'd like it if I spent some time with her too."

Susan smiled. "That's very sweet of you."

After breakfast, Mark put on some boots and a warm jacket and went outside. Connie was lying on her back in the snow, making snow angels. Mark marveled as he stepped into the snow and his foot sank ten inches. What amazing stuff, he thought.

"Ready?" Connie asked, getting up.

"Sure."

They started down the driveway and out into the road. The road had been plowed, but it was still quite narrow. A large, long mound of plowed snow lined either side of the road. There wasn't much room for two cars to pass, not to mention pedestrians.

"What happens if a car comes?" Mark asked.

"We do this." Connie scrambled over one of the mounds of snow left on the side of the road by the snowplow.

"Okay, gotcha." Mark smiled.

They continued down the road until the playground came into view. It had never occurred to Mark that kids would want to play in a playground after it had snowed. But now he could see kids on the swings and monkey bars, throwing snowballs and enjoying themselves. Mark looked around the playground. Henry was not to be seen.

Connie played in the playground all morning. A bunch of her friends showed up, and the sun-warmed winter air was filled with their laughter. The current game was to build a snowman near the swings, then get on the swing and see if you could swing close enough to kick his head off.

Not far away, Mark sat on a bench and watched. The sun warmed him as he sat guard duty. He was tired and his eyes felt scratchy, like there were tiny grains of sand behind his eyelids. He yawned and wished he could take a nap, but after Henry's threat the night before, there was no way Mark was going to let Connie out of his sight.

He was so intent on watching her that he didn't notice Alice Davenport approach until she was practically right in front of the bench.

"Hello, Mark."

Mark looked up, surprised. Alice was wearing a large navy-blue parka and white earmuffs. He suddenly remembered that at his last appointment he'd agreed to have another meeting with her.

"Susan said you'd be here," Alice said. "I guess you forgot about our appointment."

Mark looked away. He couldn't believe she'd actually come and found him. What was she going to do now? Try to have a session right there in the playground?

"Did you forget?" Alice asked.

In a way, Mark had. But there were reasons why he'd forgotten. One was that it was much more important that he protect Connie. And there was another reason.

"Maybe I just didn't feel like talking," he said.

"May I join you?" Alice asked.

Mark gave her a surprised look. He didn't want her to join him, but he knew it would be rude to say so.

Alice swept some snow off the bench and sat down. Mark stared out at the playground, but he knew she was still looking at him.

"Talking helps, Mark," she said. "It helped last time, didn't it?"

Last time, Mark thought. It seemed like a long time ago. It felt as though so much had happened since then. It was so weird. There was so much inside now that he couldn't talk about.

Or could he?

Mark turned and looked at Alice. "You're a doctor. You know things."

"Well, some things," Alice said. "I can't do brain surgery."

"But you know about people," Mark said.

"Let's suffice it to say that it's an area I'm more comfortable with," Alice allowed.

"What do you think makes people evil?" Mark asked.

Alice looked surprised for a moment. Then puzzled. "What do you mean by 'evil,' Mark?"

"I mean, someone who's bad," Mark said. "Someone who does things on purpose just to hurt other people. You know, evil."

Then Alice said something that surprised him: "Evil's a word I don't have much time for."

"What do you mean?" Mark asked.

"I believe it's what people say when they've given up trying to understand someone," Alice said.

"There's a reason for everything, Mark. And that includes people's behavior. Unfortunately, the reason can be difficult to find sometimes."

"But what if there isn't a reason?" Mark asked. "What if something just is?"

"It would seem to me that if something just is, then it must have always been that way," Alice said. "Don't you see? If it happens, then there's a cause. But if it simply exists, it has to exist from the start. Now let me ask you a question, Mark: Do you believe someone can be born evil?"

Mark wasn't certain, but it didn't seem as if it was possible. And it didn't seem as though anything Wallace or Susan would have done would have made Henry evil. He shook his head. Alice was watching him again.

"I have another question," Alice said. "Do you think you're evil? Because you let your mother die?"

Mark sighed and stared out at the playground, where a bunch of very unevil-looking kids were now playing tag in the snow. How could he explain that he wasn't talking about himself?

"It's not true," Alice said gently. "You didn't let your mother die. And you're not evil."

"Okay, but wait," Mark said. "Just listen for a second. What if there was this boy?"

"A boy about your age?" Alice asked.

Mark nodded. "Suppose he did these terrible things. . . . And the only reason he did them was because he *liked* doing them. Wouldn't you say he was evil?"

Alice gazed off at the bright blue cloudless sky for a few moments, then shook her head. "I'm sorry, Mark, but I simply do not believe in evil."

Mark had lost patience. She wasn't even listening to him. He got up and turned to her.

"So you don't believe in evil?"

Alice Davenport shook her head.

"Well, you should," Mark said. Before Alice could reply, he had jogged off through the snow toward Connie.

"Hey, Connie," he shouted. "It's lunchtime. Come on, we better go."

As Connie joined him, Mark glanced out of the corner of his eye at Alice. She was still sitting on the bench, watching him with a concerned look on her face.

The phone was ringing. Henry stopped in the entryway and picked it up.

"Hello?"

For a split second all he heard was distant static. Then a faraway voice said, "Hello? Wallace?"

"It's Henry." He was surprised the caller couldn't tell the difference in their voices. He either had to be calling from far away or was someone who didn't know them very well.

"This is Jack. I'm calling from Hong Kong."

"Oh, hi, Uncle Jack." Henry glanced up and down the hallway to make sure he was alone.

"How is everyone?" Jack asked.

"Fine, Uncle Jack. How are you?"

"Tired, but otherwise all right. I've been running like mad all week. But I wanted to call and say hello to everyone. Is Mark there?"

Henry glanced out the front window. He could see Mark and Connie coming up the street. "Mark's not here right now."

"Oh, darn. Any idea where he is?"

"Sorry, I couldn't tell you," Henry said. Outside, Mark and Connie were approaching the front walk. Henry had been wondering where they were and if they were together.

"Oh, well. So, how are things going? You kids having any fun?"

"Lots of fun," Henry replied.

"Glad to hear it," Jack said. "So, you think Mark likes it there?"

"Oh, yeah," Henry said, watching Mark and Connie start up the walk toward the front door. "I think he really likes it here. And we really like him too."

"Well, do me a great big favor and tell Mark I called, okay?" Jack said. "And give my best to your folks."

"Sure thing, Uncle Jack," Henry said. "Bye, now."

"Bye."

Henry hung up just as the front door opened and Mark and Connie came in. Their cheeks were red from the cold and they stamped their snowy shoes on the mat.

Mark froze when he saw Henry at the other end of the hall watching them. Henry stared back. Mark waited for him to say something, but his cousin remained silent. Mark turned to help Connie out of her snowsuit.

When he looked up again, Henry was gone.

16

Mark didn't see Henry again until lunch. Wallace and Susan joined them, and they ate in the dining room at the long, rectangular table. Mark sat across the table and as far away from Henry as he could. He didn't want to have anything to do with him.

"So, what's going on tonight?" Henry asked as they ate cold cuts with potato salad and cole slaw.

"I'm taking your mom out to dinner," Wallace said. "You think you characters can babysit yourselves and not get into too much trouble?"

"Sure, Dad," Henry replied with a smile.

"Oh, boy!" Connie said. "It'll be fun!"

Mark felt his stomach start to knot up. The thought of being alone in the house with Connie and Henry filled him with dread. Who knew what Henry might try to do?

"Can I stay up late and watch 'Monsterpiece Theater'?" Connie asked excitedly.

"No," Henry said.

"Why not?" Connie pouted.

"Because it might warp your impressionable little brain," Henry replied.

If the thought hadn't been so scary, it might have been funny, Mark thought. Imagine Henry warning his sister that a TV show might hurt her when she was living with a monster who could do her more harm than anything she might see on TV.

"I don't have to listen to you," Connie told her brother. "You're not the boss."

Henry's face darkened. "I am too the boss . . . vermin."

Susan's eyes widened. "That's quite enough, Henry."

"What's a vermin?" Connie asked.

"Never mind, Connie," Wallace said. "It was something Henry should not have said."

"And something he won't say again," Susan added, staring straight at her son.

Henry blinked, and Mark watched him transform himself into a friendly, smiling son once again.

"Oh, Dad, Mom," he said, "guess what? Mark's been saying that he'd kind of like to move into Richard's room."

Mark's jaw dropped. He'd never said anything like that.

"You know, that's not a bad idea," Wallace said.

Mark watched Susan stiffen. He knew that using Richard's room was a big source of disagreement between Susan and Wallace.

"Darling," Susan said to Wallace, "you know that we've been through this before."

"Mark seems to like it in there," Henry put in, as if to add fuel to the fire.

"That's not true," Mark complained. "I don't want to move into that room. I never said I wanted to."

"Now, Mark, don't lie," Henry said with a wink.

Mark's mouth opened, but no words came out. He was flabbergasted by this latest scheme of Henry's. Meanwhile, Susan and Wallace were in a deep discussion that bordered on becoming a full-blown argument. Mark definitely got the feeling that this was exactly what Henry had hoped would happen.

"Honey, I really think you should give the idea some thought," Wallace was saying to his wife. "We can't keep the room like that forever. It's turning into a museum. It's not good for the kids."

Mark could see that Susan was barely in control of her emotions. Clenching a napkin tightly in her hand, she leaned across the table toward her husband.

"I never said it would be forever," she insisted. "I'll change the room when I'm ready." She turned to Mark, who felt terrible for having any part in making her feel so bad, even though it was a lie Henry had made up.

"Mark," Susan said, "there's a nice room on the next floor you can use."

"But I don't want to," Mark said. "I never said I wanted to stay in Richard's room. Henry's making that up."

But it was as though no one had heard him.

"Listen to me, honey," Wallace said. "If Mark moved in there, it would help. The room needs to be lived in. I'm not saying you should throw any of the toys or the other stuff away."

Mark could see that Susan was on the verge of tears. She'd said everything she had to say on the matter.

"I really don't want to discuss this right now," she said.

But Wallace wouldn't let it go. "I know you don't want to discuss it. But we've got to face it. We can't keep running away."

Chair legs scraped the floor as Susan abruptly got up. She was trembling and doing everything within her power to choke back her tears. "I *am* facing it!" she cried. "Every day. You're the one who's forgetting."

Henry brought a hand to his face, and Mark was the only one who saw that he was smirking. As though he was *enjoying* this. As though he got a kick out of seeing others in pain. Mark wanted to jump up out of his chair and point at him.

See! he wanted to shout. *He's the one who's doing it! He's the one who's stirring everything up!*

But he couldn't say it. They'd never believe him.

Susan started out of the room.

"Please don't walk away from this," Wallace said, rising halfway out of his chair. "Susan, please."

But Susan had left the room, and they could hear her footsteps hurrying up the stairs. It was pretty obvious she wasn't coming back.

"Christ," Wallace muttered, lowering his head into his hands.

For a moment the room was still. Mark could hear Susan's footsteps as she reached the second floor and started down the hallway above them. Wallace also looked up. They all knew she was going to Richard's room.

Mark looked around the table. Wallace looked sad. Even Henry had managed to give himself an appropriately sad expression. Only Connie looked puzzled, as if she still didn't understand what had just happened.

"Daddy?" she said.

Wallace looked in her direction. "What is it, honey?"

"What's a vermin?" Connie asked.

Mark felt a pang for her. The poor kid was so young and innocent. Then he looked down the table, curious to see how Henry had reacted to the question. As expected, Henry had covered his mouth again with his hand. No doubt he was laughing inside.

Susan pushed open the door to Richard's room and stepped inside. She felt a tear roll out of her eye and down her cheek. It was sad, but she'd realized long ago that Wallace would never understand the way she felt. It hurt to think that he didn't feel the same way, but they were two different people, and everyone had a different way of dealing with grief. In his own way, she was sure that Wallace felt the pain of Richard's loss as deeply as she. He just dealt with it differently.

She sat down on the bed and gazed around the room. Standing on the night table was a small toy mirror Richard had gotten on his second birthday. The frame was the face of Donald Duck. Susan picked it up and gazed at it.

Then she saw something that took her by surprise. In the mirror's reflection, she was startled to see Henry standing in the doorway. She could tell that he wasn't aware that she was looking at him. On his face was the oddest smile.

It was almost contemptuous.

Almost a smirk.

Susan spun around. Henry looked surprised for a moment. Now the look on his face was one of deep sympathy. Susan could only assume that she'd been mistaken about the earlier look on Henry's face.

Her son stepped toward her and put his hand on her shoulder.

"Don't cry, Mom," he said softly.

He's such a dear boy, Susan thought. So sweet and thoughtful. At times almost more so than her husband. Almost too good to be true, she sometimes said. But this was one time when she was glad it was true. She took his hand and pressed it against her damp cheek.

"Thank you, Henry," she whispered. "Thank you for understanding."

* * *

As the afternoon passed, Mark felt a growing sense of dread over the approaching evening. He spent most of the afternoon playing with, or at least keeping an eye on, Connie. Henry came and went, but the boys said nothing to each other.

As the sun went down, Mark, Connie, and Henry ate a hastily prepared dinner in the kitchen. Connie talked about playing in the snow that day. Mark was quiet. Henry shot him a few taunting smiles, as if to say *Just wait until tonight, when my parents leave.*

After dinner, Mark sat in the upstairs hall, pretending to read a book. A few yards away, Connie played in her room with her dolls. Downstairs, Mark heard the tapping sound of leather dress shoes on the wooden floor of the entryway. Moments later, he heard the sharper click of high heels. It sounded as if they were coming from the kitchen.

"Ready?" Wallace called.

"Just a minute," Susan called back. The clicks of her heels sounded more rapidly, and Mark could actually track her movements through the rooms below. Finally Susan must have come into the entryway.

"You look fantastic," Mark heard Wallace say.

"Oh, Wallace," Susan replied with a giggle.

They were on their way. Mark jumped up and headed down the stairs. Below in the entryway, he could see Wallace helping Susan on with her coat.

"Hi, guys," Mark said, coming down the stairs.

"Oh, hi, Mark," Susan said. "I left the light on in the kitchen in case one of you gets hungry. There are plenty of things to snack on."

"Thanks." Mark dawdled for a moment, and Wallace shot him a curious glance. Suddenly what Mark had been thinking came blurting out: "Do you guys really have to go?"

Wallace smiled. "Sorry, Mark. She's my date tonight, and I'm not sharing her with anybody."

Mark glanced at Susan. He could tell that she sensed his unease. "Is something wrong?" she asked.

Mark shrugged and nodded slightly. Wallace glanced impatiently at his watch.

"I hate to say this, but if we don't leave right now we're going to lose our reservation," he said.

"Can it wait until tomorrow?" Susan asked Mark.

Mark frowned but then nodded. He didn't want to ruin their night out. Besides, how could he explain that he was afraid Henry would do something bad to Connie? Why would they believe him?

"Now, you and Henry are in charge, okay?" Susan said. "The restaurant's phone number is right by the phone. Connie's light goes out at eight-thirty. Henry knows what to do."

I'll bet he does, Mark thought.

Wallace held open the front door, and Mark felt a cold draft sweep in as Henry's parents went out on the porch. He stood in the hall, watching them, wishing they would change their minds at the last moment and decide to stay home. As if sensing his discomfort again, Susan glanced back at him with a questioning look.

"Uh, have a good time." Mark waved uncomfortably.

Susan waved back, then she and Wallace went down the steps and out the walk toward the car.

Mark stood alone in the empty entryway. The only thing that stood between a cute, innocent, six-year-old girl and her evil brother was him.

They all watched TV in the living room for a while. Every time Mark glanced at Henry, his cousin gave him a taunting look, as if he knew what Mark was thinking. Mark knew Henry was doing everything he could to increase Mark's discomfort, and he tried to steel himself against it.

At the same time, he watched every move that Henry made. At one point during a show, Henry disappeared into the kitchen for a little while. It seemed like a harmless act until Mark considered the possibilities.

A few minutes later, after the show had ended, Mark got up and said he was thirsty. He went into the kitchen and looked around. No knives appeared to be missing. No foods appeared to have been mixed with poison and left out. As a safety precaution, he wrote down the restaurant's telephone number on a second piece of paper and slid it into his pocket.

When he returned to the living room, the television had been turned off and Henry and Connie were gone.

"Connie?" Mark called.

"Up here," she called back.

Mark went to the foot of the stairs. Connie and her brother stood above him.

"Guess what we're going to play, Mark?" Connie asked, filled with childish excitement. "Hide-and-seek! And I get to hide first!"

Hide-and-seek? Mark suddenly envisioned a dozen ways in which Connie might fall into harm's way.

"No, wait," he said. "I've got a better idea."

But it was too late. Connie had already turned and was headed off somewhere on the second floor. Henry started down the steps, grinning at Mark.

"Think you can find her before I can?" he asked.

Mark was certainly going to try. No sooner had Henry reached the bottom of the stairs than Mark ran past him and started climbing up. He started to work his way down the second-floor hall, checking the rooms as he went.

"Connie!" he called. "Connie, tell me where you are. I've got an idea for a game you'll like even better."

He'd worked his way halfway down the second floor when the lights suddenly went out. Every light in the house! Suddenly Mark was standing in darkness.

17

HE PRESSED HIS HANDS AGAINST THE WALL AND FELT around until he found a light switch. He flicked it.

Nothing.

What could have happened? Was there a power failure? Mark looked out a window toward the street. No, the streetlights were on, and the house across the way had lights.

Henry must have turned off the electricity.

"Connie?" Mark called into the darkness.

"Come and get me," a voice called back. It sounded as though Connie was up on the third floor. As Mark started down the hall toward the stairs, he heard floorboards creaking and saw Henry pass through a small patch of light from the street. He was also on his way upstairs, moving quickly and stealthily.

Mark knew he had to find Connie before his cousin did. Running his fingers along the wall, he worked his way up to the third floor and stopped. A little more light came through the windows here, and Mark looked down the hall. There was no sign of Connie or Henry, just a series of closed doors.

And shadows. Creepy ones. He was starting to hate the shadows in this house.

Then Mark noticed that one door was slightly ajar. He quickly moved toward it and pushed it open.

"Connie?" he whispered urgently.

The room was almost pitch-black. The shade must have been pulled. Mark thought he heard breathing. He stepped cautiously into the room.

"Connie?" he whispered. "Are you in here?"

Suddenly a blinding light burst on, aimed directly into his eyes.

"Ahhh!" Mark gasped, stunned and frightened. He stumbled back a few steps and banged painfully into the doorway.

The beam of light flipped upward, illuminating Henry's leering face. "Oops! Sorry, Mark."

Henry aimed the flashlight toward the hall and ran out of the room.

"Where are you going?" Mark called as he followed behind him.

In the hallway, Henry stopped and aimed the flashlight at him again. "Where do you think?"

Mark knew that as long as Henry had the flashlight, he had a tremendous advantage over Mark.

"You know, it's not fair that you have that flashlight," he said.

"Not fair?" Henry looked amused. "What do you think this is, Mark? A game?"

The flashlight flicked off and the hallway went dark. For a few moments Mark couldn't see, since his eyes hadn't adjusted. But he heard footsteps as Henry raced ahead. He started to race after him, then stopped abruptly.

What if it was a trap?

Mark decided to proceed slowly. He inched his way forward in the dark, listening carefully for any sound that might give him a clue as to what lay ahead.

"Ahhhh!" A sudden, piercing scream sent a shiver through Mark. He froze in terrified confusion. It sounded like Connie, and it seemed to have come from that floor. But where?

"Connie!" Mark shouted. "Where are you?"

"Ahhhhh! Stop it, Henry!" This second scream raised the hairs on Mark's neck. Henry had gotten to her first. What was he doing to her?

"Connie!" Mark shouted again, more frantically. He started to move down the hall, pushing open doors as he went.

"Stop it, Henry!" She was up ahead. Mark turned a corner and pushed open a door. The room inside was lit by the flashlight, which lay on the floor. Mark couldn't see Henry or his sister, but he could hear sounds of scuffling. He quickly grabbed the flashlight and looked around.

There they were, writhing on the floor. What was Henry doing to her?

"Henry, stop! Stop!" Connie screamed and giggled. With a wave of relief, Mark realized what was going on. Henry was just tickling her.

They both got up. Connie had a big smile on her face. Henry was also smiling, but his was one of victorious contempt. He knew he'd scared the daylights out of Mark.

"That was fun," Connie said. "Let's play it again."

Mark couldn't stand the thought. "I think it's your bedtime."

"No!" Connie crossed her arms and stubbornly shook her head. "I want to play again."

"You heard her," Henry said. "She wants to play again."

Mark knew he had to come up with something better. "Hey, Connie, suppose I read you a story instead?"

"Only one?" Even at her young age, Connie knew how to make the best out of a deal.

"As many as you want." Mark quickly gave in.

Connie started to walk toward the door, but Henry grabbed her by the arm.

"Connie doesn't want to hear stories," he said, squeezing her arm. "Do you, Connie?"

But his little sister pulled free and ran toward Mark. "I do too . . . vermin."

It should have been a funny moment. But in the shadows cast by the flashlight, Mark saw Henry's eyes narrow into menacing slits. Almost like the look he'd given the dog a few days earlier, back at the pond. Meanwhile, Connie took Mark's hand.

"Come on, Mark," she said. "Let's go. I already know which story I want to hear first."

Connie was pulling him out of the room. Mark glanced back at Henry, who just stood there with a blank expression on his face. Mark had the flashlight in his hand and wasn't about to give it back as long as the electricity was off. He and Connie left the room, leaving Henry in the dark.

As they went down the stairs, Mark suddenly heard a loud crash. He and Connie stopped for a second. Neither said a thing. It sounded like Henry might have kicked over a chair or something.

Mark held the flashlight while Connie changed into a light blue pair of pajamas. Henry's sister was still young enough not to be self-conscious about a strange boy watching her change clothes. She got into her bed and pushed some pillows against the headboard, making a place for Mark to sit. Mark was touched by her sweet, unknowing innocence. She didn't have a mean bone in her body. It seemed incredible to Mark that Henry would want to harm her.

She got him to read three books. Somewhere in the middle of the second, the lights went back on, including a reading lamp on the night table beside Connie's bed. Mark switched off the flashlight and continued to read.

The last story was *Madeline,* a book Mark's mother had read to him when he was younger. As he reached the end of the story about the little girl at the boarding school in Paris who has an appendicitis, he could see that Connie was struggling to keep her eyes open.

"'Good night, little girls,'" Mark read quietly. "'Thank the Lord you are well. And now go to sleep, said Miss Clavell. And she turned off the light, and closed the door. And that's all there is, there isn't anymore.'"

Connie's eyes had firmly closed and she let out a deep sigh, as if letting go of the memory of that day. Mark put down the book and pulled the covers up to her chin. He gazed for a moment at her sweet angelic face, then turned off the light on the nightstand. The only light now came through the doorway. Mark walked quietly out of the room and into the hall.

Suddenly he was face-to-face with Henry, who seemed to have come from out of nowhere.

"That was a darling story, Mark," Henry said with a smirk.

Mark immediately tensed. Henry started to go around him and into Connie's room. Reflexively, Mark's arm shot out to stop him.

"What're you doing?" he asked.

"I just want to look at my kid sister," Henry replied, pushing Mark's arm out of the way. "Got to make sure she's tucked in."

"She's tucked in," Mark said, stepping into Henry's path.

"We'll see." Henry quickly faked to his right and

went left around Mark, who instantly turned and followed him into the room. Henry went to the bed and switched the reading light back on. Then he bent over his sister. Connie had fallen asleep with her head bent back and her neck exposed. Mark watched nervously as Henry reached out to touch it.

"Such a sweet little thing." Henry's words were filled with ominous mockery. He straightened up and turned toward Mark in the half-light. "Do you really think I'd hurt her?"

They stared into each other's eyes. Mark nodded slowly.

"Yes," he said.

He thought perhaps Henry would get angry, but he only smiled. As if he was proud.

Connie stirred and muttered something unintelligible under her breath. Both boys turned and looked at her. Mark felt Henry's hand on his shoulder, and it squeezed uncomfortably.

"What are you gonna do?" Henry asked. "Stay here and watch her all night?"

Mark slapped his cousin's hand away. "Yeah, if that's what it'll take, I will."

Henry stared at him with a blank expression and vacant eyes. Then he turned and left the room. Mark stayed inside and closed the door. He wished he could lock it, but there was no door lock.

Mark stepped into the middle of the room. He looked around and sighed. It looked as though he was going to spend the night on Connie's floor. He stepped closer to Connie's bed, picked up the pillow he'd leaned against while reading, and placed it on the floor. Then he lay down and put his head on it. The floor was hard and cold, and he wished he didn't have to sleep there, but he did.

* * *

Susan was aware that their dinner out was not quite the celebration Wallace had hoped for. She'd been nervous and distracted all evening long. Even a glass of wine hadn't been able to calm the sense of dread that grew in her as the evening progressed. Finally, just before dessert, she made him take her home.

"I don't get it," he said as they drove up the road toward the house. "Why do you think something's wrong?"

"I wish I could explain," Susan said. "I've just had the worst feeling all night long."

"Based on what?" Wallace asked.

"I don't know." Susan stared out the windshield anxiously, as if expecting to see the street blocked by fire engines and her house up in flames.

"This isn't like you, Susan," her husband said. "I don't mind you being upset, so long as there's *a reason* for it."

"I wouldn't feel this way if there weren't," Susan replied tartly.

Wallace sighed in frustration. "Susan, please. Try to be reasonable about this."

"I just feel like something isn't right," she said. "Call it women's intuition if you have to give it a label."

"I'm not calling it anything," Wallace replied. "I just have a feeling that you're going to get home and discover that everything is perfectly fine."

They pulled into the driveway and drove up to the house. Susan pushed open the car door and hurried up the walk. She stumbled momentarily on the porch steps, then regained her balance.

"Hey," Wallace called behind her. "Take it easy."

"I can't," Susan replied, as she pulled out her house key and unlocked the front door.

Wallace caught up to her as she opened the door.

Together they stepped into the darkened entryway. Susan flicked on the light and then stood still, listening and trying to gauge the atmosphere of the house.

"Now, what did I tell you?" Wallace asked softly. "The house is quiet. I'm sure everyone's asleep."

Susan hoped he was right, but she still wasn't certain. The anxious feeling inside her had not diminished one bit.

"Let's go upstairs," Wallace said.

"Wait." Susan walked toward the living room and turned on another light. Everything looked fine and slightly messy, which was the way she would have expected it to look after an evening of unsupervised play.

Then she noticed one of Connie's dolls lying on the rug, its legs buckled underneath it. Somehow it looked odd to her.

"What is it?" Wallace asked.

Susan held up the doll.

"Just a doll?" Wallace asked, puzzled.

Maybe it was just a doll, but somehow the sight of it instantly increased Susan's agitation. She turned and quickly left the living room, heading for the steps.

Clutching the doll, she reached the top of the steps and hurried down the hall. The door to the boys' room was wide open. It was dark inside. Susan didn't stop to look inside. Something told her everything was all right in there. She continued on to Connie's door.

It was closed tight. Susan felt the cold doorknob in her hand as she turned it. Light from the hall drifted into the room. At first Susan saw only a tangle of sheets and blankets on the bed. Then her eyes focused on her daughter and she felt better.

"What's he doing in here?" Wallace whispered, coming up behind her.

Susan looked down and was surprised to see Mark curled up asleep on the floor beside the bed. She'd been so concerned about Connie that she hadn't even noticed him. But it was strange.

"I can't imagine," she whispered back.

"Think we should move him?" Wallace asked.

"No, let's let him be." Susan went out to the linen closet and got an extra blanket. Back in Connie's room, she gently laid the blanket over Mark. Then she bent over Connie and tucked the doll under the covers beside her, surreptitiously checking, as she always did, to make sure her daughter was breathing.

A moment later she stepped out of the room, pulling the door closed behind her.

"Feel better now?" Wallace whispered.

"A little," Susan nodded. "There's just one more stop." She went back to Henry's room. The door was open, and the dim light from the hall outlined Henry's body beneath the covers, his back facing them. Susan stood for a second and gazed at him.

"Looks like he's fast asleep," Wallace whispered.

Susan backed out of the doorway, pulling the door closed behind her. Little did she know that her son was far from sleep. It was true that he lay still in his bed, but had she seen his face she would have seen that his eyes were wide open, the pupils as black as the darkest night.

18

MARK OPENED HIS EYES. HE WAS LYING ON THE FLOOR IN A room filled with light. A blue wool blanket covered him. For a moment he wasn't certain what he was doing there. Had he fallen out of bed?

Then it all came back to him in a rush. The memory of the night before.

He sat up. Connie's bed was empty and unmade. Where was she?

Henry.

A sudden panic gripped him as he jumped up. He was just about to dash out of the room when he heard a young girl's voice coming from outside. Mark stepped to the window and looked down. Outside, wearing her pink snowsuit and a white hat, Connie was talking cheerfully to herself as she built a snowman.

Mark smiled to himself and felt a wave of relief. She was all right.

For now.

A little while later Mark went down the stairs, pulling on a blue sweater. He intended to grab a quick bite of breakfast and then go outside on the pretext of helping Connie with her snowman. He got to the bottom of the stairs and started for the kitchen. But now he heard new voices: strained, emotional voices. Through the doorway ahead he could see Wallace with his arm around Susan. Susan's head was bent. Her voice was sad.

"I can't explain it," she was saying.

"Is it Richard's room?" Wallace asked gently.

"That's part of it."

"Look, I don't care about the room," Wallace said. "If it helps you somehow to leave it the way it is, then fine."

Susan looked up at him. "Are you sure?"

"Yes," Wallace said. "But there's more to it than that. You've got to stop blaming yourself for Richard's death. It wasn't your fault."

"But I left him alone in the tub," she said.

"In six inches of water," Wallace said. "It was a freak accident. He was sitting there in the tub and the phone rang. You did what anyone would have done. You told yourself no two-year-old could possibly drown in six inches of water, and then you went to answer the phone. I would have done the same thing."

"But you didn't," Susan said. "I did."

"It was a freak accident, honey," Wallace said. "You can't go through life blaming yourself."

"I do," Susan said. "No matter how I try to rationalize it, I still do. I just can't forgive myself."

"You've got to," Wallace said. "Look what it's doing to us. We can't even go out and enjoy dinner together anymore."

"I know." Susan leaned into him and pressed her forehead against his shoulder. "I'm sorry, I really am. I don't mean to be like this. I don't mean to push you away. It's just so difficult."

"I know it is." Wallace slid his arms around her and

looked up at the kitchen clock. "Sweetheart, I have to go."

"You sure?" She grabbed the sweater he was wearing and held it tight.

"You know I wouldn't go if I didn't have to," Wallace said. He gave her a hug. "I love you."

"I love you," Susan replied, her voice a strained whisper.

From down the hall, Mark watched Wallace turn and leave. Six inches of water, he thought. That's what Richard drowned in. He tried to imagine what a two-year-old looked like. They weren't really babies anymore. People called them toddlers instead. They walked pretty certainly and had almost complete control of their bodies. He'd heard stories about how little water it took to drown in. Maybe a baby could drown in six inches of water. A baby that couldn't yet push itself up into a sitting position.

But a toddler?

Henry.

Mark tried to shake the thought from his mind. It was a terrible, awful thought. And yet, if there was anyone in the world who could do it, it was Henry.

Mark walked slowly toward the kitchen, hoping that Susan would have had time to pull herself together. She had turned away and now faced the kitchen sink with her head still bowed. Mark stopped, then made a couple of loud stepping sounds in place to warn her that he was on his way.

Susan's head snapped up. She turned and looked at him. A smile came to her lips, but it came slowly and seemed forced.

"Morning, Mark."

"Morning."

"Want some breakfast?"

Mark shook his head. "I'm not too hungry. But thanks."

"You slept in Connie's room last night."

"Yeah." Mark could feel her eyes on him. He wondered if she was waiting for some kind of explanation, but nothing immediately came to mind.

"Are you okay, Mark?" she asked.

He looked up. "Why do you ask?"

"You seemed pretty anxious last night."

He nodded. That weird feeling was coming back. The feeling that they were connected somehow, that they communicated on their own private wavelength that no one else was on.

"Do you want to tell me what it was about?" Susan asked as she poured water into the coffee machine.

"Well . . ." Mark did want to tell her, but how? How did you tell a mother that her son was a crazy, vicious, evil person?

"You don't have to, you know."

Mark wondered if she was trying reverse psychology. No, he decided, in her case she really meant it. He didn't have to say anything if he didn't want to. But he did.

"It's about Henry." He started cautiously, waiting to see how she'd react.

"I thought so." Susan nodded. "I've picked up on some tension between you two."

"Yeah." Tension was a pretty mild way of describing it, actually.

"Is everything all right?" Susan asked.

"No, not really." Mark looked around the kitchen and back down the hall.

"You can speak up," Susan said. "Henry's not in the house."

A second of relief was followed quickly by sudden apprehension. "Where is he?"

"He went out with Connie."

Mark quickly went to the window and looked outside. The snowman Connie had been working on was standing by itself: two stones for eyes and a short, crooked branch for a nose.

"Out?" Mark felt a rising panic.

"Yes," Susan said. "Actually, Henry was very cute about it. He said they weren't spending enough time together."

Oh, God! Mark thought. His heart began to race.

"I think he's a little jealous that you and Connie—" Susan started to say, but Mark quickly cut her short.

"Where'd they go?" he asked desperately.

"The quarry."

"Why? What's there?"

"Ice-skating," Susan replied. "Why? What's wrong, Mark?"

"I can't explain," Mark gasped. "Where is this quarry? How do I get to it?"

"Go to the end of the driveway and make a left," Susan said. "Follow the road about a hundred yards and then make a right down Quarry Lane. You'll see it."

"Thanks." Mark exploded out of the kitchen.

"But wait!" Susan yelled behind him. "What's the rush?"

Mark had no time to answer. Within seconds he'd thrown on boots and a jacket and had raced outside.

The air was cold, and as Mark ran great plumes of vapor trailed behind him with every escaping breath. He quickly found Quarry Lane and started down it. Soon he came to a path through the woods where the snow had been trampled down hard. A dozen yards ahead of him three girls in brightly colored parkas walked along with ice skates thrown over their shoulders.

Mark dashed past them. Ahead, through the bare brown trees, he could see a rise that led to a ridge. With his heart beating wildly, Mark ran up the incline. At the top he stopped to catch his breath. Below him was a wide abandoned quarry, flooded and covered with ice. There must have been a hundred people, mostly kids, skating on it.

Mark strained his eyes for a sign of Henry and Connie, but there were too many kids in pink snow-suits and white hats. It was impossible to see.

But he had to find her . . . had to warn her before it was too late.

"Connie!" he shouted, and he started to run again. "Connieeeee!"

His shouts were lost amid the voices and laughter below. Once again Mark started to run, this time down the slippery slope toward the ice. As he got closer, the bodies gliding along the ice became more distinctive. His eyes began to pick out young couples and older boys skating with younger girls.

"Connie!" Mark shouted. The frantic run was exhausting him. He had to stop and rest. He staggered up to a tree and leaned on it, gasping in the chilly air. Where was she?

Was he already too late?

The quarry was broad and long, with a slight bend in the middle. Most of the skaters were to Mark's left. But now he saw a pair break away from the main crowd: A boy wearing a navy-blue cap, a blue jacket, jeans, and black hockey skates was pulling someone smaller, someone wearing a pink snowsuit and a white cap. They were still too far away for Mark to see their faces.

But he knew. He just knew.

"Connie!" he shouted at the top of his lungs. *"Connie, wait!"*

There was no sign that she heard him. The boy—it

had to be Henry—was pulling her, and she held on to one of his hands with both of hers, as if she was water-skiing. As they left the crowd of skaters, Mark could see that Henry's head was down and his free arm was swinging as he strained to pick up speed.

"Connie!" Mark launched himself from the tree trunk and started running again. The downhill slope became steeper as he veered off the beaten path and crashed through the unbroken snow, blundering through trees and underbrush with one hand over his face to protect himself from the bare slashing branches.

"Eeeeeeeiiii!" Now he could hear Connie's screams, a mixture of delight and terror, as Henry raced faster and faster, pulling her toward the bend in the quarry. Ahead a tall jagged rock wall prevented Mark from seeing what was on the other side.

"Ooof!" Mark crashed through some bushes and stumbled onto the ice.

"Hey!" "Look out!" "Interference!" A dozen voices were yelling at him all at once. Mark found himself in the midst of a dozen guys with hockey sticks. He'd stumbled into a hockey game!

"Sorry! Really, sorry!" Mark gasped and propelled himself forward on the ice. The soles of his boots slipped and slid, but gradually he picked up speed.

He had to get around the bend. He had to see what was on the other side.

Far out on the ice, Henry had started swinging through a long arching curve. Connie was bent at the waist, as if it took all her strength to hold on to her brother's hand.

"Connie, let go!" Mark shouted as he scrambled farther out onto the ice. Now he could see what was

out there: a thin wooden barrier painted red and white, warning skaters of thin ice ahead.

Henry was skating in a wide arc toward the barrier. As he started to curve around, Connie swung to the outside of the arc. Suddenly Henry heaved her forward and let go. Like a slingshot, Connie rocketed toward the red and white barrier, her small body wobbling back and forth, her arms flailing in the air as she tried to keep her balance.

She crashed through the barrier and fell forward onto her stomach, still sliding. Her arms and legs were splayed in all directions, but there was nothing to hold on to. Nothing to stop her.

Ahead of her the ice turned from white to dull gray, and Mark could see a thin layer of water on the surface.

Connie slid toward the gray spot . . .

And then disappeared.

"Oh, my God, Connie!" Mark screamed. He tried to run faster, but he felt almost like a cartoon character: The faster his legs spun beneath him, the slower he went.

Out beyond the barrier, Connie's head, still covered by the white cap, bobbed to the surface.

"Connie!" he screamed again.

His screams began to attract attention. Now other skaters were pointing toward the broken barrier. People began to shout.

"Look! Someone's fallen in!"

"Get help!"

In an instant the entire crowd had stopped skating and was watching. To Mark's surprise, Henry was skating back toward the spot where Connie now bobbed in the frigid water. Henry stopped, bent down, and began to crawl on his stomach over the ice toward his sister.

Now the skaters began to move toward the barrier. Once again Mark was left behind and had to stumble over the ice to catch up. What was Henry doing? he wondered. Was he really trying to save her?

Ahead he saw Connie raise her arm in a slow, lethargic motion: hypothermia, the loss of body heat. He'd read about it somewhere. She had to be feeling it.

The skaters had started to venture beyond the barrier. Mark could see Henry looking back over his shoulder at them.

"Don't come too close!" Henry shouted at them. "The ice is breaking!"

Mark saw Connie's head disappear from sight.

"I can't find her!" Henry was screaming. "I can't find her!"

Mark was still trying to make his way through the crowd. Suddenly there were new shouts behind him.

"Out of the way!" "Make way!"

He spun around and saw two men skating toward him. One was carrying a long metal ladder, the other a sledgehammer.

Suddenly there was a loud *crack!* beneath everyone's feet.

"What was that?" someone shouted.

"The ice!" someone else yelled. "It's cracking!"

"Too much weight in one place!" the man with the ladder shouted. "Get back, all of you! Get back and spread out!"

The crowd instantly began to back away and spread out. The two men continued out onto the thin ice.

The man with the sledgehammer gave it to the man with the ladder. "It's too thin!" he yelled. "You'll have to go it alone!"

Now the last man continued across the ice toward

Henry, carrying both the sledgehammer and the ladder.

It's taking too long! Mark thought, still working his way through the watching skaters. Finally he reached the broken barrier and started through it. Suddenly a hand landed on his shoulder, halting his forward progress.

Mark turned and saw the man who'd been carrying the sledgehammer.

"I have to help," Mark gasped.

"You can't go out there," the man snapped.

"But she'll drown!"

"So will you."

Out on the ice the man dropped to his hands and knees and slid the ladder toward Henry. The crowd around Mark had been murmuring, but now it quieted. On the ice, Henry turned and saw the man was on the ladder, crawling toward him.

"She's not there!" he shouted.

"Go back!" the man shouted.

"But . . ."

"Go back along the ladder, now!"

Henry started back along the ladder. Still on his hands and knees, the man with the sledgehammer crawled as close to the broken ice as he could get.

"What's he doing?" someone in the crowd near Mark asked.

"Looking for her."

"But she's not there."

"She went under. She could be anywhere."

In the distance, Mark heard an ambulance siren approaching. His throat felt constricted. His heart beat like mad. No, he told himself. It couldn't happen.

Not again.

Not to Connie.

Suddenly the man out on the ice grabbed the sledgehammer and swung down hard. White chips of ice flew into the air as the head of the sledgehammer sank in. Tossing the sledgehammer to one side, the man threw himself on his stomach and reached down. His arms disappeared under the ice.

A moment later a white hat appeared. Then he pulled Connie's limp, wet body out.

"He found her!" someone yelled.

Some of the skaters actually began to cheer. Meanwhile, the man out on the ice bent over Connie and began to give her mouth-to-mouth resuscitation.

"Was she under too long?" someone near Mark asked.

"It wasn't more than a minute," the man holding Mark said.

"Does that mean she has a chance?" Mark asked.

"Yes," the man replied. "A chance."

"Emergency Services is here!" someone shouted.

Mark turned and saw a man and woman hurrying toward the edge of the ice, carrying a stretcher and an oxygen tank. The man out on the ice with Connie saw them. He lifted Connie in his arms and, still giving her mouth-to-mouth resuscitation, skated quickly toward the shore.

The crowd watched as the man handed Connie to the Emergency Services people. They quickly strapped her to the stretcher and put the oxygen mask on her, then hurried back down the path through the woods.

"They've stopped the CPR," someone said. "They're giving her oxygen. She must be breathing."

Mark felt a weak wave of relief sweep over him. Around him, some people started skating again. Others had had enough excitement for one day and headed toward shore.

Henry, Mark thought. He looked around and saw a

small crowd of people surrounding someone on a rock on the shore. As he walked in that direction, he replayed in his mind what had just happened. Had anyone else seen Henry pulling Connie toward the barrier? Yes, but they'd probably thought it was just two kids fooling around. Even to Mark, Henry's actions had been hard to decipher. It looked so much as though they were just having fun, as though Henry had been pulling Connie along for fun and had simply lost control out near the barrier.

If it had been any other kid, Mark would have automatically assumed it was an accident.

But it wasn't any other kid.

It was Henry.

Now he knew why Henry had gone back to the hole after Connie had fallen through.

It wasn't to save her.

It was to watch.

The way he'd stared at the dead dog.

The way he'd watched the accident.

The way he'd asked Mark if he'd seen his mother after she'd died.

The way he'd said he'd taken a good look at his brother Richard after he'd died.

He liked to see death.

As Mark neared the small crowd, he could see that Henry was at the center of it. Someone had thrown a blanket over his shoulders, and someone else was crouching down in front of him and talking. Henry's head was bowed, and he nodded every once in a while.

What a great actor, Mark thought. It took all his self-control not to push through the crowd and smash his fist into his cousin's face.

Mark stepped closer. Now Henry looked up and spotted him. For a moment the two boys just stared at each other. Mark could almost see the crooked, knowing smile. But it wasn't on Henry's lips.

It was in his eyes.

"It's all right," someone near Henry said, laying a comforting hand on his shoulder. "Your sister's going to be all right."

Henry nodded and looked down at the ground.

As if he was sad. As if it had all been an accident.

Mark clenched his fists, then turned and walked away.

19

SUSAN HAD BEEN IN THE LIVING ROOM. SHE'D BEEN STANDING by the piano, looking at the photograph of Richard. He'd been a strong boy for his age. Already steady on his feet. How could he have drowned?

It was a question she'd asked herself almost every day, almost every waking hour, since the terrible thing had happened.

She, Henry, and Richard had been alone in the house that day. Wallace had taken Connie to the store. She'd left Richard sitting up in the tub, playing with his bath toys.

When she came back, he was facedown.

In six inches of water.

And that left Henry. . . . Susan shook the thought from her mind. No, she mustn't think that. She mustn't. It was an awful, terrible thing to think. It simply couldn't be true, and she hated herself for even considering it. No, Richard's death was a freak accident. Just like Wallace had said.

In six inches of water.

And then the phone rang. It was Wallace. He'd been in town when someone he knew grabbed him and told

him what had just happened down at the quarry:
Connie had fallen through the ice while skating. The
Emergency Services people had taken her to the
hospital.

From that second on, Susan hadn't stopped moving. She'd grabbed her coat and catapulted herself out
of the house and into the car. She'd raced to the
hospital, ran across the parking lot, dashed up the
steps, and burst through the front door, her coat flying
behind her.

All she could think was one thing: *Not again.*

Oh, please, God, don't let it happen again.

She'd cursed the elevator all the way up to the
fourth floor, then ran out and flew down the corridor,
dodging patients on walkers and in wheelchairs.

Ahead, Wallace stepped out of a room, talking to a
doctor in a white coat with a stethoscope hanging
around his neck. Hearing the rapid approach of her
footsteps, he turned.

For a split second Susan searched his face for news.
Oh, please, God, please!

A small, grim smile appeared on Wallace's face.
"She's going to be okay, Susan."

Susan's knees turned to Jell-O. Suddenly weak with
relief, she crumpled into her husband's arms.

Thank God!

The man who'd stopped Mark from crossing the
barrier gave him a ride to the hospital. Mark had
explained that he was the cousin of the girl who'd
almost drowned. The man knew Henry because he
had a son the same age and they'd been on the same
soccer team the year before.

"He was a mighty brave boy," the man said as they
pulled into the hospital parking lot.

Mark nodded and didn't say anything. If only they
knew.

By the time Mark got to Connie's room, Wallace, Susan, and Henry were already there. Mark assumed that one of those sympathetic people who'd comforted his cousin had brought him to the hospital. He just hoped that Susan and Wallace would be so distracted by what had happened to Connie that it wouldn't occur to them to ask why he and Henry hadn't come together.

The door was open, but Mark knocked lightly on it anyway. Wallace looked up.

"Come in, Mark," he said.

Mark entered the room. Henry was sitting close to Susan. She had her arm around him. Connie lay in the big hospital bed, her eyes closed, fast asleep. Near her a small green monitor emitted blipping sounds as it tracked her heartbeat.

"She's okay?" Mark asked.

"Yes, she's going to be fine," Wallace said.

"Great." Mark felt relieved. He sat down in an empty chair in the corner and gazed at Connie. She'd been lucky. Very, very lucky. But he should have been there sooner. He never should have let her go off alone with Henry.

"Mark?"

He turned and saw that Susan was looking at him. "Yes?"

"You went to the quarry, didn't you?"

An apprehensive feeling swept over Mark as he nodded.

"Did you see what happened?"

Mark's lips parted. He didn't know what to say.

"I don't think he got there until later," Henry said.

Mark knew it was the wrong time to say something. Susan reached up and smoothed Henry's hair appreciatively. "What you did was very brave. You saved your sister."

Mark watched Henry smile and drink in his mother's adoration. If only she knew.

Afternoon visiting hours ended. Just to be safe, the doctor insisted that Connie remain in the hospital overnight. It was still daylight when Mark and the others got home. Susan got out of the car, but instead of going inside, she said she wanted to take a walk.

Henry went into the house. Wallace went up the porch steps and held the door for Mark.

"You coming?"

Mark shook his head. "I think I'll go for a walk too."

"Okay, see you in a bit." Wallace let the front door close.

Mark looked around behind the house. He could see Susan's back as she walked. He knew she was going out to her spot on the cliffs above the ocean.

He had to tell her. But what if she didn't believe him?

Why *should* she believe him?

Because he was telling the truth.

But what proof did he have?

Mark started to follow her. It didn't matter what proof he did or didn't have. He had to tell Susan now, before Henry had a chance to hurt Connie again.

A late-afternoon wind had kicked up. The bare tree branches swayed and creaked, and the snow blew into drifts. Mark's hair was whipping around. Ahead, Susan stood at the edge of the cliffs, looking down at the rough waves crashing on the rocks below. Suddenly she turned as if she'd sensed him behind her.

"What are you doing here?" she asked. The question wasn't angry, just curious.

"I have to talk to you," Mark said.

She stared at him for a moment. "Something's wrong, isn't it? You wanted to tell me last night."

Mark nodded. Would she believe him?

"Tell me what it is," Susan said.

"Henry said I wasn't at the quarry, but I was."

Susan just watched him, telling him to continue with her eyes.

"Well, I can't say for sure," Mark said, feeling a great nervousness inside. "I mean, I wasn't that close, but . . ."

"But what, Mark?" Susan brushed the blowing hair out of her eyes.

"I . . . I don't think what happened was an accident," Mark said.

"What?" Susan's forehead furrowed.

"There wasn't anyone else at that end of the quarry, because the ice was too thin," Mark said. "Henry was pulling Connie. They were going way too fast. And then he sort of let go. . . . I mean, he sort of threw her at the thin ice."

Susan blinked.

"He told me he hated her," Mark said.

Susan stepped closer to him. "What are you trying to tell me?"

"It wasn't an accident," Mark said. "That's why I ran out of the house when you told me they'd gone to the quarry. I knew what he wanted to do."

"What did he want to do?" Susan asked.

It was so hard for Mark to say it. How could she ever believe it? She was Henry's mother. And yet he knew he had to say it.

"Connie didn't slip," Mark said. "It was Henry. You don't know what he is. He tried to kill her."

"No!" Susan shouted. Her hand flew out, smacking Mark across the face.

Mark staggered backward as the burning sensation radiated out from his cheek.

"You're wrong!" Susan shouted at him, almost out of control. "You're lying. Henry's my son. I love him, and nothing you say will ever change that. He's my little boy. He's my son. Don't ever come to me with these lies again."

She spun around and hurried off. Mark watched her through the tears in his eyes. He brought his hand up to the tender, stinging skin on his face. She didn't believe him. She'd *never* believe him.

Mark started to walk slowly back to the house. It was hopeless. No one would believe him . . . not until it was too late. Not only that, but he'd now lost the only ally he had here. Suddenly he felt very alone. More alone even than when his own mother had died.

It took Susan a while to calm down. As the sun went down and she stood by the window in her bedroom, she wondered what had prompted Mark to say what he had. It was such a horrible thought, such an outrageous thought.

And yet, deep inside, it triggered something in her. Something that went back to earlier that afternoon, when she'd stood by the piano and looked at the photograph of Richard. The same thought had flickered briefly in her mind before she'd snuffed it out.

Six inches of water.

And now Mark had relit it. She was sorry that she'd struck him. But everything else she'd done was right. She had to deny it. There was no evidence. Henry was her son, for God's sake. He was a good boy, a sweet boy.

And yet, wasn't it strange that she and Mark had both had that thought?

Susan suddenly had an overwhelming urge to go back to the hospital. She just wanted to be with Connie. She didn't want her daughter to be alone.

Bleep! Bleep! Bleep! The only sounds in the dark hospital room came from the heart monitor and the breaths Connie took in her sleep. The only light came from the thin green line on the monitor that jumped with every heartbeat. Susan sat in the corner behind the door, just listening. She knew she had to be there, but she wasn't sure why. Strange thoughts ran just below the surface of her consciousness, like fish in a dark sea. She knew they were there but she couldn't see them.

Or was it that she didn't want to see them?

Suddenly the door cracked open, letting a shaft of light in. Susan almost said something, but a voice in her head told her to be quiet and still.

The door opened farther. In the light from the hall, Susan saw Henry step into the room. Without turning on the light, he walked quietly toward his sister's bed.

What was he doing here? Susan wondered. Why hadn't he turned on the light? Her hands gripped the arms of the chair tightly as she watched Henry walk to the side of the bed and hover silently over his sleeping sister. Then he slowly turned and gazed at the heart monitor. The reflection of the blipping light was like a line of war paint across his darkened face.

Why was he staring at it like that?
What strange fascination did it hold for him?
Suddenly, Susan felt afraid.

"Henry?"

Henry spun around, his surprised expression caught in the light of the lamp Susan had just switched on. For a brief instant he looked like a deer caught in the headlights of an oncoming car. But then he quickly recovered his composure and smiled his most charming, boyish smile.

But the smile disconcerted Susan.

"Mom, I didn't see you."

"Shhh, don't wake your sister." Susan brought a finger to her lips and quietly got up. "What are you doing here? I thought you were home with Dad."

Henry turned back to the bed and gently brushed a strand of hair out of Connie's eyes. "I was worried about Connie," he said softly. "Did she wake up yet?"

"She was up for a little while before," Susan said. "She seemed very confused."

"About what?" Henry asked just a shade too quickly, as if he was worried about something.

Susan reluctantly registered her son's reaction. "About why she's in the hospital. I don't think she remembers much about what happened."

Was it her imagination, or did Henry appear to sag slightly with relief?

"That's good," he said. "It's probably better if she forgets all about it."

Susan watched him closely, a feeling of extreme discomfort percolating just below the surface. "Henry, what *did* happen at the quarry?"

Henry looked puzzled. "I told you, Mom, it was an accident."

"Of course." Susan nodded and forced a slight smile on her face.

Henry's face suddenly became sad. "I know I've always treated her like a bratty kid sister. But until today . . . I never realized what she meant to me."

Susan regarded her son for a moment. She'd seen him act this way before. So sweet, so earnest, even remorseful. Sometimes he truly seemed too good to be true. Now she had to wonder. There was the other night when he'd come into Richard's room. She remembered the glimpse she'd gotten of him in that little mirror. It was a glimpse of a different boy. The same boy she'd just seen slip into the hospital room, believing he was alone.

Was it possible that he was acting? That this was all an act? A slightly sickening sensation threatened to invade her, and she chastised herself for thinking that way. No, it couldn't be. He was her *son*.

And yet . . .

"Does Dad know you're here?" she asked.

"No, I sneaked out," Henry said. "Guess I should have told him, huh?"

"Yes."

"Well, I better get home before he notices," Henry said. "You coming?"

"In a while," Susan said. "You run along."

He turned toward the door. Susan felt the questions still nagging her. It simply didn't all add up.

"Henry?" she asked.

"Yes, Mom?" He spun around and faced her. Was there something guilty in his movements? Something overly self-conscious? Or was she just imagining it?

Henry gave her an open, innocent look. Susan changed her mind. It couldn't be. No twelve-year-old could be *that* evil and conniving.

"Never mind," Susan said. "I'll see you back at home."

Henry nodded and took one last look at Connie. "Tell her I was here, okay?"

"I will."

Henry smiled and left the room. Susan could hear him go back down the hall, whistling.

20

IT WAS MIDDAY IN MAINE, WHICH MEANT IT WAS SOMETIME in the middle of the night in Japan. Mark was supposed to leave for Alice Davenport's soon. He was mad because Susan had mentioned the appointment in front of Henry that morning. Then Henry had given Mark that grin, like he knew a secret. Like he was superior or something because Mark had to go see a shrink and he didn't. That was the cruelest irony of all to Mark. Because if ever there was a kid who needed to talk to a shrink, it was Henry.

It was almost time for the appointment, but Alice Davenport could wait. Mark had been waiting all morning for a chance to use the phone. Now he snuck into Wallace's study and dialed the phone number his father had left him. He had to be quiet. Susan had gone to get Connie from the hospital, but Wallace and Henry might still be around.

There were a couple of strange beeps and buzzes, then the phone rang for a long time. Mark was just about to give up when a woman answered the phone. Mark couldn't understand a word she said. She had answered in Japanese.

"Uh, do you speak English?" Mark asked in a hushed voice.

"How can I help you?" the woman replied in English. Mark thought he heard her yawn.

"I'd like room four twenty-seven, please."

"One minute, please."

More clicks. Then the phone started to ring again. Mark waited impatiently, worried that Wallace or Henry would walk in any second and discover him. Why wasn't his father answering, anyway? It was supposed to be the middle of the night over there.

"Hello?" a groggy male voice answered the phone.

"Dad?"

"Mark?"

"Yeah. Look, I'm sorry I woke you."

"Oh, uh, is something wrong? Are you all right?"

"Dad, you've got to come back here," Mark whispered.

"Wha . . . Why? What's wrong?"

"It's Henry," Mark said. "He's doing things. Bad things. Terrible things."

"What do you mean by 'terrible things'?" his father asked.

"He's got everybody fooled," Mark said. "They think he's a great kid, but he's really evil."

"Whoa, Mark, you're going too fast for me. Did you say 'evil'?"

"Yes."

"How?"

"He killed a dog with a machine he made that shoots railroad spikes. He caused a car accident that could have killed a whole bunch of people. Then yesterday he tried to kill Connie."

"What? Kill Connie? Mark, is Wallace there? Or Susan?"

"Dad, you have to listen to me," Mark pleaded. "I

tried to tell them, but they won't believe me. No one will, but it's true."

"What about Alice Davenport?"

Mark sighed. "I haven't told her, Dad. She thinks I'm just some screwed-up little kid."

For a moment the phone line went quiet. Mark could just barely hear the faint traces of another conversation occurring somewhere in the world.

"Mark," his father said, "when is your next appointment with Alice?"

"It's today," Mark said, his voice etched with disappointment. If his father was asking about dumb Alice Davenport, it meant he wasn't going to come home.

"I want you to tell Alice what you told me," his father said. "Do you understand?"

"Yeah, sure." Mark made sure his father heard the disappointment in his voice.

"Good."

Mark had the feeling his father wanted to hang up and go back to sleep.

"Dad?"

"Yes, Mark?"

"When do you think you'll come back?"

"Soon, Mark. As soon as I can."

"Do you believe me, Dad?"

When his father hesitated in his answer, Mark knew he probably didn't.

Then, instead of answering, his father said, "I'll be back as soon as I can."

"Hurry, Dad, okay?"

"I'll try."

"Promise?"

"Yes, Mark, I promise. I'm going to try to get back to you as soon as I can."

"Thanks, Dad. And I'm really sorry I woke you."

"It's okay, Mark. Just make sure you tell Alice Davenport everything you told me. It's important."

They said goodbye and hung up. Mark could tell his father wasn't certain whether to believe him or not. But at least he'd be home soon. Mark needed him.

A little while later, as Mark walked up the path to Alice Davenport's house, he went over in his head what he wanted to tell her. He'd start from the very beginning. If he had to, he'd try to get her to find the man who owned the dog Henry had killed. And maybe he could get her to talk to the police about the car accident and Mr. Highway.

Preoccupied with these thoughts, Mark entered the house. The doorway leading to Alice's office was open. He could hear voices coming from inside. That was strange. Mark was certain it was time for his appointment. He heard Alice laugh.

Mark stepped into her office and froze. Someone was already sitting in the chair. His back was to Mark, but Mark had no doubt who it was.

"Mark, I'm glad you're here," Alice said with a smile.

Henry leaned out of the chair and also smiled. "Hi, Mark."

Mark couldn't believe it. How? Why? But the answers were too obvious. Henry was there to foil his plans. The kid was not only evil, he was smart.

"Come in, Mark," Alice said. "Sit down."

Mark didn't move. He just glared at Henry. "What are you doing here?"

"Please, Mark," Alice said. "Henry's here because he wants to help. He says you two have been having some problems."

Mark looked up at her incredulously. *"He's* the problem!"

"Now, Mark, please," Alice said gently. "As you know, there are always two sides to every story. Why don't you sit down and we'll all try to solve this with an open mind."

Mark already knew what that meant. Henry was too wily for him. He was too good at winning.

"Forget it," Mark said. "You're already on his side, aren't you?"

Alice frowned. "I don't take sides, Mark."

"Yes, you do," Mark spat. "I heard you talking and laughing. He's got you fooled, just like everyone else."

"Mark, please," Alice said, drawing from her endless supply of patience. "No one's here to fool anyone."

"Oh, give me a break!" Mark turned and stormed out of the office, slamming the door behind him.

"Mark, wait!" Alice called after him.

The front door slammed.

"Oh, dear." Alice appeared to deflate slightly.

"Sorry," Henry said. "I didn't mean to cause trouble."

"It's not your fault," Alice said with a sigh. "Mark is having a tough time. He's going through some very difficult times."

"Is he . . . okay?" Henry asked.

"What do you mean?" Alice asked.

"Well . . ." Henry shrugged and fidgeted in his chair, as if he was uncomfortable.

"What is it, Henry?"

"I don't know if I should tell you."

"Well, it's up to you, Henry," Alice said. "But it's clear that I'm having a hard time getting through to Mark. Anything you could tell me might help."

"You sure?" Henry asked innocently.

"Yes."

Henry took a deep breath and let it out slowly.

"Well, it's just the way he acts when no one's around. Sometimes he really scares me."

"How? What does he do?"

Henry slumped a little in his chair and bit his lip. He wanted to appear very uncomfortable. "I don't think I should tell you."

"Why not?"

"Because Mark's my friend. I mean, even though we've had some fights, I still like him."

"Except when he scares you," Alice said.

"Well . . . yeah."

Alice leaned forward. "Listen to me, Henry. Anything you tell me about Mark will help him, not hurt him. You won't be betraying him. You'll be helping him. Please, Henry, tell me everything."

"Everything?" On the outside, Henry furrowed his brow as if he was terribly conflicted. But inside he was smiling. He then proceeded to tell Alice everything he wanted her to know.

Mark sat in the treehouse. There were still no walls or roof, and he could see the clouds slipping past above. He had to think, had to figure out a way to deal with Henry. So far he'd been honest and Henry had been deceitful. And who was winning? Henry.

Maybe it was time to change.

He could hear breathing. Looking down over the edge of the platform, he saw Henry climbing up toward him. A few moments later Henry was grinning at him as he pulled himself onto the platform.

"You sure missed an interesting session," he said with a teasing smile. "You know, I think I like therapy."

"What did you tell her?" Mark asked coolly.

"Sorry, that's strictly confidential," Henry replied. "But you'd better stop telling lies about me, because no one's going to believe you."

"They're not lies," Mark said. "We both know that."

"Prove it." Henry said. He wasn't smiling anymore.

"Sooner or later, they're going to find out about you," Mark said. "You can't get away with this stuff forever."

"Who's 'they'?" Henry asked. "My mom? My dad?"

"I told your mom."

Henry didn't appear to be the least bit worried.

"So? Why would she believe you? She's my mom, not yours."

Mind games, Mark thought. That's what he does. So do it to him.

"You're wrong," he said. "She's my mom."

Henry screwed up his face. "What are you talking about? Your mom's maggot food."

"I said, she's my mom." Mark got up. Henry followed his lead. The two boys faced each other on the platform.

"Before she died, my mom gave me a sign," Mark said. "She promised me she'd come back. I didn't know how she'd do it, but now I do. She chose your mom. You wouldn't understand that, Henry. But she's my mom now."

He could see he'd gotten to Henry. The kid was scowling at him uncertainly. Mark had said it just to get Henry going, but the strange thing was, as soon as he said it, he knew it felt good. It felt right. He wanted Susan to be his mom. He wanted her, and she deserved a better son than Henry.

Meanwhile, Henry stared at him uncertainly. "You're crazy, Mark. You know that?"

"She's my mom, Henry," Mark said confidently, moving past him to the edge of the platform. "That's just the way it is."

Mark eased himself over the edge and down to the

first branch. Above him, Henry stuck his face out over the edge of the platform.

"Mark," he said, as cold and serious as Mark had ever seen him.

"What?" Mark snapped back confidently.

"Don't mess with me," Henry said.

Mark just gave him the most charming smile he could and started to climb down.

21

IT WAS NIGHT. THE WIND WHISTLED THROUGH THE TREES and drove the loose snow into drifts against the house. The naked branches of the trees scraped and tapped against the windows like skeletal fingers.

In his bed in Henry's room, Mark suddenly awoke and looked around. In the dark he could see that Henry's bed was empty. He was up to something, Mark was certain of it. The thought made his stomach knot. He wanted to stay in the warm safety of his bed, but he couldn't. He slipped out of his bed and went out into the hall.

Dull, refracted rays from the streetlights dimly lit the hall. Those shadows again . . .

Moving slowly, eerily . . .

Mark was really starting to hate them.

He stood quietly in the hall. Henry could have been anywhere in the house, doing anything. Mark decided to check on the others first. As he walked down the hall, the streetlights cast more thick, threatening shadows on the walls.

It was spooky. He wished he were back in bed. But he'd never sleep now. Not with Henry on the loose.

He stopped outside Susan and Wallace's room and listened for a moment.

Nothing.

Mark slowly opened the door. It was dark inside, but he could see their outlines under the blankets. Wallace snorted and mumbled something in his sleep. Mark got the feeling the room had not been disturbed. He backed out and tried Connie's room next. Susan had brought her home that afternoon, and she'd quickly returned to her normal little-girl self, playing and laughing and fighting with Henry as if the awful trauma of the day before had been forgotten.

Connie too appeared to be fast asleep and undisturbed.

So where was Henry? Mark went back out into the hall. The idea of that kid out there loose and unseen frightened him. He could feel his heart rev up nervously, and even though it was cold in the house, a worried sweat broke out on his forehead.

He stood at the top of the stairs and listened. At first he heard nothing but the wind and the trees against the windows, but then a slight clinking sound caught his ear. It wasn't the sound of tree branches against glass. It was the sound of *glass* against glass.

It seemed to be coming from the kitchen.

Mark started down the stairs and soon stood in the kitchen doorway. The refrigerator door was open, casting an eerie glow over the room. Mark looked around for Henry, but he was nowhere in sight. Cautiously, he stepped to the refrigerator and looked inside.

Everything appeared normal.

"Looking for a midnight snack?"

Mark jumped around and found Henry behind him, his face awash in the pale light from the refrigerator.

"Go ahead," Henry said. "Eat, drink. Don't let me stop you."

Mark stared at him, waiting for his heart to slow. He swallowed, then looked back into the refrigerator. Henry was up to something. He was sure of it.

"What did you do?" Mark demanded.

"Do? Me?" Henry asked with faked innocence. "Oh, I get it: You think I put something in my family's food."

Mark quickly glanced into the refrigerator and then back at Henry again. "Did you?"

"Hey, Mark, come on," Henry replied with a smirk. "Do you really think I'd do something like that?"

It could be a trick. With Henry you never knew.

That was the problem.

Mark reached into the fridge and pulled out a container of orange juice. He opened the top and sniffed it.

It smelled like orange juice, but what did he know? He had no idea what poison would smell like.

What if it wasn't a trick?

He couldn't take a chance, not with Henry.

Mark quickly flicked on the kitchen light and rushed to the sink. He emptied the orange juice into it.

There. It was gone.

He turned and looked at Henry. The kid stood there with his arms crossed and a smug look on his face as he shook his head.

Then it hit Mark: Henry had poisoned something else as well. Mark stared back into the open refrigerator. It could be in anything. *Anything!*

There was only one thing to do. Mark went back to the refrigerator, grabbed a carton of milk and a plastic container of cottage cheese, and placed them on the counter next to the sink. Then he grabbed a bottle of apple juice and a container of leftover spaghetti sauce.

It could be in anything!

Before long he'd emptied the entire refrigerator and stacked its contents on the counter beside the sink. Next he started to pour all the liquids into the sink. Some of them splashed onto his pajamas, but he didn't care. He started the garbage disposal and began to open the containers and dump their contents in. Bits of food and sauces splattered around the sink and on the counters and on his clothes.

Some stuff had to be scraped out. Mark grabbed a wooden spoon and started scraping. The mustard, the ketchup, and all the jellies disappeared down the disposal, but not before Mark had managed to get quite a bit on his clothes.

"Mark!"

Mark looked over his shoulder. Susan and Wallace stood in the doorway, looking sleepy, but surprised. Henry stood behind them, with a phony look of concern on his face.

"Oh, Mark!" Susan came toward him and grabbed his shoulders, pulling him away from the sink. "We want to help you. I know how much you miss your mother. I know it's hard for you. . . ."

They didn't get it. They didn't get it at all! They thought he was upset about his mother!

Mark pointed at Henry, who hung back near the refrigerator.

"You don't understand," he said. "It's Henry! He's trying to poison you!"

Susan's face fell. She looked sick at heart. "Mark, please . . ."

They didn't believe him. They thought *he* was the crazy one. Meanwhile, Henry was playing it perfectly. He tugged on his father's sleeve and spoke in a frightened, little-boy voice.

"Dad?" he whimpered. "I'm scared. Does he have to stay in my room?"

Mark could see Wallace waver and glance at Susan questioningly. Wallace stepped toward Mark and placed his hand on his shoulder. "Come on, Mark," he said, his voice etched with disappointment and just a trace of annoyance. "We'll get you cleaned up."

Mark backed away. "You don't get it. You really don't. He tried to kill Connie. He made it look like he was trying to poison you. I had to throw everything out. I couldn't take the chance—"

"That's enough!" Wallace snapped sternly. "You get yourself to the bathroom. Now!"

Mark knew he had to obey. As they walked toward the bathroom, Mark tried to explain. It was no use. Wallace wasn't interested in knowing how Henry had tried to poison his family. Finally Mark just shut up.

Wallace waited outside the bathroom while Mark washed and changed into a clean pair of pajamas. Then they went into Richard's room. Mark dreaded sleeping there. There was something eerie about the room and how it was filled with the things of a dead little boy. Mark sat down on the little bed and looked back at Wallace, who stood in the doorway and yawned.

"We'll talk in the morning," Wallace said.

"What for?" Mark asked, boiling with frustration. "Nobody believes me."

Wallace gave him a funny look and then closed the door. Mark wouldn't have been surprised if he locked him in. He felt totally defeated. When it came to being devious, Henry was the champ.

Susan waited in the hall outside her bedroom for Wallace to return. Her arms were crossed tight with worry. The hallway was filled with swaying, ominous shadows from outside. It was odd how she'd never noticed them before.

"How is he?" she asked as her husband came back to their room.

"I don't know what to tell you," Wallace replied. "He seems very angry."

"How do you explain the kitchen?" Susan asked. "And his story about Henry trying to kill Connie?"

"I can't," Wallace said with a sigh. "I wouldn't even try."

"What are we going to do?" Susan asked.

"Jack will be back in a few days," Wallace said. "Let's just try to keep it together until he gets here."

Wallace started to go past her into the room, but Susan put out her hand to stop him. "Wait."

"What?"

She could see he wanted to get back to bed, but there were still things on her mind. "Why would he think Henry poisoned the food?" she asked.

"I'm not a mind reader," Wallace replied, shaking his head.

"But . . ."

"We can talk about it in the morning," Wallace said, stepping past her and into the room.

As Wallace left the hallway, Henry came into view, standing by his door. Susan hadn't seen him before because Wallace had blocked her view. Obviously, he'd been listening to their conversation. Now he stood there with a smile on his face. He was smiling like a host who'd just thrown a wonderful party. It jarred Susan.

"Henry, go to bed," she said.

Henry quickly ducked back into his room. Susan turned and stepped into hers, but she was deeply troubled by what she'd just seen. Why had Mark behaved like that? And why had Henry been smiling? Odd memories flashed back into her mind. The way she'd seen Henry smile in the mirror when she'd sat in

Richard's room. The way he'd snuck into Connie's hospital room and stared at the heart monitor. The whole issue of Connie's near drowning still disturbed her. She may have been young, but she was a sensible child. Why would she have skated past the warning barrier? Why hadn't Henry tried to stop her?

Susan got into bed and lay in the dark, staring up at the ceiling. Next to her, Wallace had begun snoring again, but Susan knew there'd be no sleep for her that evening. Something about Henry was bothering her deeply.

She knew Janice's death must have been incredibly upsetting to Mark, but why would he say what he'd said about Henry?

Why would he say Henry had tried to drown Connie?

Why would he think Henry wanted to poison them?
Six inches of water.

22

THE NEXT MORNING SUSAN WENT OUT TO THE GARAGE where Henry did his "experiments." She hadn't been in there in years. Some time ago Henry had taken over the garage. He'd never said she couldn't go in there, and yet at the same time it was understood that this was Henry's private domain. Susan really hadn't given it much thought. It seemed like a game, like the whim of a small, innocent boy.

But after the events of the past few days, she was starting to wonder. Driven by a dark suspicion she didn't quite understand, she pushed open the door to the garage and stepped inside.

The room was cold and still. It was filled with odd-looking devices and boxes of loose mechanical parts. Of course, Susan had seen the things Henry had built in his bedroom, but these were stranger, darker. She didn't understand them.

She stepped around them carefully, like a visitor in a museum. She didn't want to disturb anything.

Something strange stared up at her from a box on the floor. She picked it up. It seemed to be a mask of some sort, made out of a small lampshade. It seemed odd, but not so odd that she should worry about it. She was putting it back when she noticed something else in the box. She reached in and pulled out a small toy rubber whale.

It had belonged to Richard.

A very uncomfortable feeling spread over Susan. After he'd died she'd practically turned the house upside down looking for it. She'd never understood why. It was just something she'd wanted to have. What was it doing in Henry's things?

"Mom?"

It was Henry's voice. Like a child caught with a hand in the cookie jar, Susan spun around and hid the whale in a pocket of her coat.

Henry stepped into the garage, carrying a plastic sled under his arm. His cheeks were red from the cold.

"What are you doing in here?" Henry asked with a strange calmness. Susan saw his eyes dart around as if he was looking to see if she'd disturbed anything.

"I was just looking around," Susan said. She hated the thought of lying to him, of being deceitful. And yet somehow, it seemed necessary.

Henry put his sled down, then walked over to his workbench and began to hang some tools on a pegboard. He seemed remarkably self-possessed.

Too self-possessed.

Susan cleared her throat. "Henry, if something was wrong, you'd tell me, wouldn't you?" She moved close and put her hand on his shoulder, but Henry moved away. He seemed to be looking for a certain tool.

"What do you mean?" he asked.

This wasn't easy for Susan. "Well, sometimes . . . when we're children . . . we do things. . . ."

"What kinds of things?"

"Things we feel bad about," Susan said.

Henry turned and looked at her. "I don't feel bad about anything."

There was no hesitancy in his voice. He appeared to be answering honestly. Susan reached into her coat pocket and took out the toy whale.

"What about this?" she asked.

Henry's expression went blank. He looked almost stunned. "Where'd you get that?"

"You know where I got it," his mother replied.

Henry turned away. Deeply puzzled and hurt, Susan stepped toward him. "I couldn't find it after Richard's accident. You took it, didn't you? You've had it all this time."

Henry muttered something Susan didn't understand.

"What did you say?"

Henry looked up at her. "I said it was mine before it was his."

The reply surprised Susan. It was such an insignificant thing. Just a little toy.

"But you knew I was looking for it," she said.

"So?"

Susan's feelings were in a jumble. She felt hurt, worried, and scared. It was hard to sort through everything. Then she realized what was bothering her the most.

"How did you get it?" she asked.

Henry shrugged and didn't answer.

"Answer me." Susan's voice became strident. She needed an explanation from him badly. "It was in the tub with Richard. How did you get it?"

Henry gave his mother an innocent look. "I took it."

"You took it?" Susan was still puzzled. "When? How?"

Henry looked contrite. "I'm sorry, Mom. I took it because . . . I wanted something to remember Richard by."

She could remember Richard playing with it in the

bathtub. Of course when she came back and found him facedown—*in six inches of water*—she'd forgotten about it. But later, much later, when she replayed the scene in her mind, she couldn't remember seeing it. When had Henry taken it?

When?

Henry held his hand out toward the rubber toy. "Could I have it back, please?" he asked sweetly.

"No, you can't have it back," Susan replied coldly. She didn't want him to have it. There was something horribly, horribly wrong here. She watched in amazement as Henry's eyes narrowed into mean slits.

"It's mine," he hissed.

"Henry . . ." Susan took a step backward. She didn't understand it at all. She didn't understand how he could act like this, changing from one second to another. It scared her. He was only twelve years old.

"Give it to me!" Henry grabbed the toy and tried to pull it out of her hands, but Susan held on tight. For a second it was a tug-of-war. Then Henry violently ripped it free and pulled it tightly to himself.

Susan stared at him, breathing hard, not comprehending. Henry stared back, his face strange, blank, guarded.

"Who are you?" she blurted out.

Henry smiled faintly. "I'm your son," he replied.

Before Susan could respond, he had turned and left the garage. Susan stared after him, horrified by what had just happened and what it could mean.

The toy whale . . .

Richard . . .

Six inches of water . . .

No, she told herself, Henry couldn't have. He was her son. Richard's big brother.

He simply couldn't have done it.

* * *

Henry stepped out of the garage and into the sunlight. The glare from the snow was almost blinding. He felt the rubber whale in his hand and looked down at it. A moment ago he'd wanted it so badly, but now it frightened him.

Richard . . .

He had to get rid of it.

He took off, running through the woods and snow as fast as his feet would carry him. The woods were a blur around him. He took in the cold air in long, hard gasps. The toy felt as if it was burning in his palm.

He had to get rid of it.

He ran through the snow, through the bare branches and brush. He made it to the cemetery and ran straight to the well. Yanking the cover off, he stared down into the darkness below for a second, then hurled the toy in. He waited and waited, then there was a faint splash.

Henry sagged against the wall, out of breath. There, it was gone. He didn't have it, his mother couldn't get it.

It was as though it had never existed.

Susan was in the car. It was too big in her mind now, too strong to push away. As she drove down the road toward Alice Davenport's, she couldn't get rid of the thoughts and suspicions she had about Henry. She could only hold them at bay by telling herself she might be wrong.

There might be an explanation.

There *had* to be!

But she was almost certain the toy whale had been gone when she went back into the bathroom and found Richard.

The whole family knew she'd looked for it.

Richard's drowning might have been a freak accident, but she knew now that Henry had very probably been in the bathroom while she was on the phone.

And if he'd done what she was afraid he had, then Mark could have been right about what Henry had tried to do to Connie.

And then Mark's bizarre behavior at the refrigerator the night before began to make sense.

No, she told herself, it couldn't be. It was impossible. She and Wallace were good parents. They'd always done the best for their children.

She couldn't possibly have given birth to such a creature.

Alice was holding the front door open for her. Susan had called ahead and warned her that she was coming over. It was a matter of extreme urgency, and she had to speak to Alice immediately.

"Are you all right?" Alice asked as Susan stepped past her and into the house.

"No." Susan walked straight down the hall and into Alice's office. From there she could look out the picture window at the ocean. It was almost like standing at her spot on the cliffs.

"Susan, what is it?" Alice asked, stepping into the office and closing the door. "What's wrong? Is it one of the boys?"

Trying to compose herself, Susan took a deep breath. She didn't want to ask the question. She was terrified of what the answer might be. But she had to ask. Still facing the window, she spoke in a soft, controlled voice.

"Tell me, Alice: Is it possible for a child to be born . . . I don't know . . . with part of him missing?"

"What do you mean?" Alice frowned.

Susan knew she'd done a poor job of asking. She might have been talking about an arm or a nose, for all Alice knew. She turned to the psychologist.

"I mean, is it possible for a boy to be incapable of feeling certain things?" she asked. "Like emotions? Like guilt? . . . Or remorse?"

"It is possible," Alice replied carefully. "But it's quite unusual."

"But suppose it happened," Susan said. "Would you be able to recognize a child like that?"

"It would be difficult," Alice said. "Such children learn very early how to duplicate emotions without really feeling them. In fact, they often appear more normal than 'normal' kids."

"Too good to be true," Susan muttered to herself in horror. Then it *was* possible. Suddenly Susan knew she couldn't avoid it. There was too much evidence now. The pieces fit together too well.

"I've been practicing for twenty years and I've never run into a child like that," Alice cautioned her, as if trying to second-guess Susan and prevent her from reaching any conclusions. "I've only read about them."

But Susan knew what Alice was doing. This was different. The evidence . . . was all there.

"Alice, I've got to run," she said, turning toward the door.

"Wait," Alice said.

"I can't. I'll call you later. I promise." She opened the door and started to go out.

"Susan, Mark isn't one of those children," Alice said behind her.

Susan stopped for just a second. "I know," she said. Henry had everyone fooled. She had to go home.

It was impossible to keep an eye on all the potential victims, so instead Mark quietly kept an eye on the potential perpetrator. He'd watched Henry go sledding that morning. Later he'd seen him go into the garage and then come running out, heading off toward the cemetery.

Now he stood quietly in the hallway outside Henry's room. Inside, Henry stood before a full-length mirror attached to his closet door. Mark couldn't figure out what he was doing. For the longest time Henry just stood there, staring at himself. Then slowly, amazingly, a tear appeared in his right eye and ran down his cheek.

Henry responded with a smile.

He's trying to make himself cry! Mark thought.

Suddenly Henry turned, and the two boys faced each other.

"What were you doing?" Mark asked.

"I'm missing someone."

"Who?" Mark asked.

Instead of answering, Henry turned back to the mirror and stared at himself again. "When you went to your mom's funeral, did you cry?"

"Why do you want to know?" Mark asked.

"I don't know," Henry said with a shrug. "I just figured you're expected to cry at your mom's funeral, that's all."

Your mom's funeral . . .

Now Mark understood. He stepped into the room. "You wouldn't."

"Wouldn't what?" Henry asked innocently.

"Hurt her."

"Do you really think I'd hurt my own . . ." Henry started to ask. Then he caught himself and smiled. "Oh, wait."

"What?" Mark asked.

"I just remembered," Henry said. "She's not my mother anymore. She's yours. Isn't that what you said? She's your mother now?"

"Yes," Mark said.

"Your mother, my mother, what the hell." Henry winked. "I guess we'll both miss her."

Mark was close now. Close enough to grab Henry by the throat and choke him. "I'll kill you first."

"Poor Mark," Henry said with a teasing tone. "So violent. So disturbed. You better watch out or they'll lock you up."

It reminded Mark of the night before, at the refrigerator. It was too real. Mark could see how Henry would do it. How he'd make sure Mark got blamed for everything.

Something inside Mark snapped. He lunged forward, grabbing a screwdriver from the workbench with one hand and grabbing Henry with the other, shoving him hard against the wall.

"I could kill you now!" Mark cried, waving the screwdriver at him.

Henry offered no resistance. Instead, he smiled back calmly. He tilted his head back and pointed at his bare throat.

"Go ahead, put it right there," he whispered. "Right where my finger is."

It wasn't a taunt. It wasn't even a dare.

Henry wanted him to do it.

Like he didn't care . . .

"Go on," Henry whispered. "You gotta push pretty hard, though. The blood'll go right across the room. Come on. Come on! Do it!"

Mark trembled. He knew he couldn't do it. No matter how evil the kid was, he just couldn't.

Suddenly Henry's eyes went to the doorway.

"Dad!" he shouted. "Dad! Help me!"

Mark just had time to turn his head. Wallace was coming toward him. The next thing he knew, Wallace had grabbed him by the collar and yanked him away, knocking the screwdriver out of his hand.

"What the hell do you think you're doing!" he shouted, shaking Mark hard. "Answer me. What's going on here?"

Mark was speechless. It was no use. Henry had won again. Now Henry came up from behind.

"It's okay, Dad," he said. "Really. I'm not hurt. Don't be mad at Mark. He's really not himself."

Mark stared past Wallace at Henry. Wallace was too busy glaring at Mark to see the big smile on Henry's face. He was loving every minute of it!

"This is serious," Wallace told Mark. "You could have hurt Henry badly."

"He's the one who wants to hurt people," Mark said. Even though he knew Wallace would probably never believe him, he couldn't stop. Henry was going to try to kill Susan!

"Come with me." Wallace took him by the arm and roughly led him toward the door. Henry followed, still playing the part of the innocent victim.

"I'm sorry you don't want to be friends, Mark," he said.

Mark stared back at Henry. There was that phony charming smile again. It *would* drive him crazy, Mark thought. He had to keep fighting. Digging his feet into the hallway carpet, he looked at Wallace pleadingly.

"Please, you've got to believe me," he begged. "He's going to do something. He said he'd—"

Wallace yanked him along. "That's enough! I'm going to get Alice Davenport over here and then we're going to talk. In the meantime, you're going to behave. Understand me?"

Mark nodded. Wallace would never believe him. He'd have to try something different. He could feel Wallace's grip on his arm start to loosen. As soon as Wallace let go of his arm, Mark bolted away. He had to get away. He had to get to someone—*anyone*—who would believe him.

Mark got to the top of the stairs and was about to run down when he found Connie in his way. Before he could get around her, Wallace had grabbed him again.

"All right!" Wallace shouted. "If that's the way you want it." The next thing Mark knew, Wallace half carried and half dragged him down the stairs.

Connie followed with a frightened look on her face. "What's wrong, Daddy? Did Mark do something bad?"

"He's just a little confused, that's all," Wallace replied, trying to sound calm for his daughter's sake. "Everything's going to be fine."

"No, it isn't," Mark yelled, trying to twist out of his grip. "You've got to listen to me!"

But Wallace didn't listen. He got Mark down the stairs, then carried him down the hall and put him in his study.

"I'm doing this for your own good," Wallace said.

The next thing Mark knew, Henry's father had pulled the door shut. Mark heard a click and knew he'd locked the door. *His own good* . . . If Wallace only knew what irony there was in his words. Mark immediately attacked the door with both fists.

"Wait!" he cried, banging as hard as he could on the door. "You've got to let me out! He's going to kill her! Don't you understand?"

No one answered.

No one understood.

23

MARK DIDN'T KNOW HOW MUCH TIME HAD PASSED. He paced the study like a caged animal. Henry was out there somewhere. Susan was out there somewhere. And he was trapped. If he didn't do something soon, Susan was going to get hurt.

He heard a car pull into the driveway. Going to the window, he looked out and saw Susan get out. Finally! She was his only and last chance. She was the only one who might believe him! But then Henry came out from around the side of the house and started talking to her.

"Oh, no!" Mark gasped. He watched as they spoke. Susan looked upset and shook her head at something Henry said. Good, Mark thought. But then Henry said something else. Susan hesitated, then nodded. Henry took her hand and began to lead her away.

"No!" Mark screamed. "Don't go! It's a trick! It's a trick!"

He banged on the window and tried to open it. It went up a few inches and then stopped. Burglarproofed! Mark ran to the door and started to pound on it with his fists. "Uncle Wallace!" he screamed. "Uncle Wallace!"

Susan walked with Henry out toward the back. A few moments ago he'd met her in the driveway with a boyish smile and announced his new plan to clean out the garage and get rid of all those strange contraptions.

But Susan angrily cut him short. She wasn't buying the act anymore. She was almost certain of what he'd done, although she still wasn't certain what, if anything, she could do about it.

After all, he was her son.

She told him they had to talk. Once and for all she had to get to the bottom of it. She had to find out the truth.

Henry had asked if they could take a walk out back, the way they used to when he was little. Susan agreed. The whole thing was breaking her heart. Besides, what harm could come from a walk in the back?

In final desperation, Mark picked up a stool and hurled it at the window.

Crash! The window shattered into a million tiny shards, sparkling in the sunlight. Mark was just trying to climb through the window when the door flew open and Wallace ran in, followed by Alice Davenport. Mark tried to throw himself out the window, but Wallace grabbed him.

"You gotta let me go!" he cried. "He's gonna kill her!"

But Mark couldn't move. Wallace restrained his arms and legs while Alice kneeled down in front of him.

"We're here now, Mark," she said in her most soothing voice. "Nothing bad is going to happen."

"No, you don't understand!" Mark struggled, but Wallace was too strong. "You don't understand!"

"We'd like to understand," Alice said patiently. "But we can't as long as you fight us. You have to promise you'll sit quietly and talk to us."

Mark stopped struggling and stared at her. He had to do whatever it took to get out of Wallace's grip. There was no time left to try to explain. By the time he did, Henry would probably have killed Susan.

Alice looked past Mark and nodded at Wallace.

"I'm going to let you go," Wallace said, breathing hard from the exertion of restraining Mark. "But you've got to promise me you won't run, okay?"

"Yes," Mark said.

He felt Wallace's grip loosen. As soon as he was free, he made a mad dash for the door. Alice tried to block his path, but he got around her. He got out into the hall and ran like mad for the front door. Just as he got there it swung open. Mark skidded to a stop.

He couldn't believe what he was seeing: his father, in a wrinkled raincoat, holding a suitcase in one hand and a briefcase in the other.

"Dad!" he cried, throwing himself at his father.

"Mark!" Jack could see that something was wrong, but right now he just wanted his son in his arms.

Mark could hear footsteps race down the hall behind him and stop.

"Jack," Wallace said. "Thank God you're here."

"What's going on?" Jack asked.

"I'm afraid it's pretty bad," Wallace said.

"Mark's in a very confused state right now," Alice tried to explain. "He tried to hurt Henry."

"Dad . . ." Mark whispered and tugged at his raincoat. His father looked down at him.

"Is that true?" Jack asked, scowling.

"No way, Dad," Mark said, still clinging to him. "There isn't anything wrong with me."

"There is, Jack," Wallace said.

"Don't listen to them," Mark said.

His father stared at him. Except for looking a little excited, Jack could see nothing wrong with the boy.

"Remember what you said before you left?" Mark asked. "You said you knew I'd be okay because you believed in me. Well, you've got to believe in me now. You've just got to!"

"Jack, you haven't been here," Wallace said. "You can't imagine what's going on."

"You've got to trust me, Dad," Mark whispered. "It's not what it seems. They've all been tricked."

Jack was quiet for a moment. He knew his son. He knew he wasn't one to make things up. Then he hugged Mark again.

"I believe in you. I always have," he said. Then he looked at Wallace and Alice. "There's nothing wrong with my son."

"I've got to go, Dad," Mark gasped. "I've really got to go!"

"Don't let him," Alice said.

Jack looked at Alice and then at Mark.

He let Mark go.

Susan and Henry walked along the path that led to the cliffs. Susan's heart was heavy and sad. Besides Richard's death, this was the worst thing that had ever happened to her. But no matter what, she couldn't give up on this child.

"I love you," she said, squeezing Henry's hand. "No matter what happens . . . no matter what you've done . . . I'll stand by you."

Henry only nodded quietly. She wondered what he was thinking. A strong wind off the ocean blew into their faces. Susan knew she had to ask the terrible question.

"Tell me the truth, Henry," she said. "Tell me what happened the night Richard died."

"Don't you know?" Henry asked innocently.

"I'd like to hear it from you," Susan said.

"I was downstairs playing . . ." he began.

Susan knew he was lying. She knew by the tone of voice he used. He used it every time he lied to her, and he'd lied to her many times.

"Don't lie to me," she snapped angrily. "I'm sick and tired of your lying."

She found herself shaking him by his shoulders. "Henry, tell me the truth: Did you kill Richard?"

Henry pulled away and regarded her coolly. It was a look that was unnatural in a boy of his age. "So what if I did?"

Susan lost her breath. She felt as if someone had just hit her in the stomach. She hardly knew what to say.

"We'll . . ." she began, but the words trailed off.

"What, Mom?" Henry asked, oddly detached.

"We'll get you help," Susan said.

"You don't look too good, Mom," Henry said. "I think you're the one who needs help."

Susan told herself that his answer was just a defense mechanism. But she had to get through to him. "You have to trust me, Henry."

But the boy shook his head. "I don't think I can. You want to send me away, don't you?"

"No . . ." Susan stammered. "I don't know . . ."

"You want to put me in one of those places," Henry said with unnerving certainty.

"No, Henry . . ."

"I'd rather die!" he shouted at her. "You hear me? I'd rather be dead!"

He turned and started to run toward the cliffs.

"Henry!" Susan started to run after him. She watched as he disappeared over a crest of land. *"Henry!"*

Susan reached the cliffs. There was no sign of her son. Assuming the worst, Susan stepped to the edge of the cliff and looked down. Suddenly she heard someone behind her. She spun around and saw her son step out from behind a gnarled tree. His expression was controlled and unemotional. Not at all what Susan had expected after he'd dashed away from her a few moments ago.

"You really thought I was going to jump?" he asked.

Susan didn't know what to say. She didn't understand what he was doing behind her.

"I guess you don't know me very well," Henry said ominously.

He was moving toward her with his arms out. Susan could hardly believe her eyes. This couldn't be happening. He couldn't be doing what she thought he was doing.

And then it was too late. He pushed her backward and she tumbled over the cliff.

She screamed and twisted around. Somehow she managed to grab onto the edge of the cliff. Her feet were hanging in the air.

"Henry!" she screamed as she clawed at the dirt and grass.

"Coming, Mother." He came to the edge of the cliff and looked at her. Her grip was giving way.

"Please!" she gasped, reaching toward him with one hand.

Henry gazed at her outstretched hand impassively. A moment later her grip gave way and she fell.

She went only a few feet and then hit something hard. Susan looked down and realized she'd landed on a narrow ledge. Below her was a two-hundred foot drop to the rocks and the waves. Her heart beat wildly. She was so terrified she could hardly move. She stared up. Henry's face poked out over the ledge and he stared down at her. There was no expression on his face. He might just as well have been looking at a rock.

"Henry . . ." Susan pleaded. She lifted her arms up toward him, but he made no move to help her. She couldn't understand it. She was so bewildered and terrified that it was difficult to move. Her tongue felt thick and heavy. It was almost impossible to get words out, but she managed a few.

"Please . . . I'm . . . your . . . mother."

Henry smiled slightly and shook his head. Then he disappeared.

"Henry?"

Nothing.

The ocean crashed beneath her. Susan looked down again, and this time she was overcome by waves of vertigo. She gasped in terror and flattened herself against the cliff.

She heard something and looked up. Above her, Henry had reappeared with a rock the size of a football.

"Henry, please . . ."

Henry raised the rock over his head. It was obvious what he was going to do. Susan cowered.

Suddenly a figure grabbed Henry from behind. The rock slipped out of his hands and fell toward Susan, but she had time to twist out of the way. The rock crashed onto the ledge she was standing on and bounced off into empty space.

It had missed her!

Susan's split second of relief was followed by instant terror as the ledge beneath her feet began to crumble under the rock's impact. She screamed as an avalanche of rock cascaded away, leaving her standing on a ledge now hardly larger than her own two feet.

On the edge of the cliff above, Mark and Henry wrestled on the ground, punching each other with their fists.

"I won't let you hurt her!" Mark shouted.

Henry grabbed him by the shoulder and they rolled dangerously close to the cliff's edge. They were face to face now, each breathing hard.

"How's it going to feel to lose two mothers?" Henry hissed.

Mark responded by punching him in the face.

Below, on the ledge, Susan began a perilous ascent. Hand over hand, grabbing every little fissure and bump, she slowly pulled herself back over the edge of the cliff.

Ten feet away, Mark and Henry wrestled and rolled within inches of the edge of the cliff. Henry managed to get on top, trying to push Mark's head back over the edge. Mark held tight, trying to pull him down.

"Mark! Henry!" Back on solid ground, Susan scrambled toward them. Just as she reached them, they began to topple over the cliff together. Susan dove forward and both boys grabbed for her. Mark grabbed her right arm and Henry grabbed her left.

"Oooff!" Their weight pulled Susan down onto her stomach. Suddenly both boys were hanging in the void, each clinging to one of Susan's arms. Susan looked down into two desperate faces. Below them was nothing but two hundred feet of empty space. And then waves crashing onto rocks.

Henry hung onto Susan's clenched left hand. Mark held onto the upper part of her coat arm. Susan felt as though their combined weight would pull her arms right out of her shoulder sockets. She pulled with all her might, but it was no use. She couldn't pull them both up at the same time.

She stared back down at them. Mark's face was etched with desperation and fear. Henry's was frighteningly calm.

What could she possibly do?

With all the charm and boyish beauty he could

muster, Henry looked up at his mother and said, "Mom, Mom . . . I love you . . . Mom, I need your other hand."

Susan felt herself slipping. She could feel that it would only be seconds until they all went over. She looked from one boy to the other with no idea of what to do.

"I'll try to pull you both!" she shouted desperately. "Hold on!"

Again she tried to pull them both up, but it was impossible. Together, they weighed too much. Meanwhile, Mark was beginning to slip. The stitching on the arm of her coat was starting to unravel under his weight.

Henry still had a firm grasp on her left hand.

Susan looked back and forth from boy to boy. Mark's eyes were growing wider in terror as the stitching on her coat continued to loosen and pull apart. His mouth was open in a silent cry, his breaths short and rapid.

Henry's expression was sweet and imploring.

How could you? it seemed to ask. *I'm your son!*

Rrriiipppppp . . . The sleeve of her coat—with Mark still hanging from it—began to give.

He was starting to slip down her arm.

In another second he'd be gone.

Susan looked from one boy to the other.

Mark . . .

Henry . . .

Her son . . .

Her choice . . .

Mark . . .

Henry . . .

Richard . . .

The toy whale . . .

Six inches of water . . .

Susan suddenly jerked her hand out of Henry's grasp and grabbed Mark, stopping his slide.

Henry's eyes went wide with surprise.

Susan looked away.

Henry plummeted downward, his arms and legs spread like a sky diver's. With a sickening smack he hit the rocks below and bounced off of them like a ragdoll. A wave crashed over his body. A moment later he was gone.

In grim, despairing silence, Susan pulled Mark back over the edge of the cliff to safety. They lay on the ground, and he clung to her, reliving the terrible near-death moments over and over. Susan clung to Mark in utter, unspeakable misery.

She'd done the worst thing a mother could do.

And she knew it was right.

24

One Year Later . . .

THE NEW RED JEEP CHEROKEE PULLED INTO THE DRIVEWAY
of the Maine house. Inside, Mark turned to his father
and gave him a questioning glance. Jack put his hand
on Mark's shoulder.

"It's all right," he said. "Everything's all right."

They got out of the car. Wallace stepped out of the
house and hugged Mark. "It's good to see you again."

Then he turned to Jack. The brothers shook hands.

"Read about your latest deal in the paper," Wallace
said. He wore a grim expression, but there was pride
in his voice.

"They made it sound better than it really is," Jack
replied.

"Don't be modest." Wallace slapped his brother on
the back. "It's amazing what you've done in just one
year. You've really turned that company around."

"I had a good year," Jack admitted. "I just wish you
could have had one too."

Wallace glanced away.

Now Connie came running around the side of the
house. She was taller and thinner, and becoming very
pretty.

"Mark! Mark!" she cried joyfully. "I saw you coming. I saw you two whole blocks away!"

Mark caught Connie in his arms and hugged her. "How'd you do that? With X-ray vision?"

"No, I saw you from the treehouse." Connie pointed to the trees behind the house. Mark could see the treehouse. It had walls and a roof now.

Mark remembered something and started to reach back into the Jeep. "I brought you something, Connie. A puzzle we can do—"

Before he could finish, Connie started to drag him away. "Come see the treehouse."

But Mark hesitated. There was something he had to do first.

"Where's your mom, Connie?" he asked.

Connie let go of his hand. She was suddenly somber. "She went to see him."

Mark nodded and looked past her toward the cemetery. "You won't be mad if I go see her, will you? I promise I'll come back and then we'll play."

"Okay, but hurry," Connie said.

Mark started off. His father caught his eye and Mark thought he might say something. But Jack only nodded solemnly.

Henry had been buried on a hilltop under a tall tree whose branches reached up toward the sky. Mark found Susan there, holding a bunch of yellow flowers in her hand, crouching beside the small gray tombstone. On the ground was a tangled bouquet of dead brown flowers.

Mark slowly crouched down beside her. Susan glanced at him with watery eyes. She didn't seem surprised to see him, but then she'd known he was coming to Maine with his father to visit. All she did was nod. She didn't have to talk. Neither did he. They knew that they shared a bond. It had begun before Henry had died, and Henry's death had only strengthened it.

Mark reached toward her and took the yellow flowers. He put them down and took away the dead ones. Then, together, he and Susan rose. They stood together for a long time, looking down at Henry's grave.

"No matter what, I still love him," Susan said, wiping a tear out of her eye with her finger.

"We'll never forget him," Mark said.

"Never." Susan's voice was barely a whisper.

Mark slid his hand into hers and looked up at her. She was his mother now. Or as close as he was ever going to get again. As if she'd read his mind, she smiled a little.

"Come on," she said. "Let's go home."

They turned and started back toward the house. Mark carried the dead brown flowers. Susan carried her memories and grief.

Behind them they left Henry and the tombstone, which read:

HENRY EVANS

1981–1993

WITHOUT DARKNESS

THERE CAN BE NO LIGHT

About the Author

Todd Strasser has written many award-winning novels for teens and adults. Several of his works have been adapted for the screen, including *Workin' for Peanuts, A Very Touchy Subject,* and *Over the Limit,* which he adapted himself. A former newspaper reporter and advertising copywriter, Strasser worked for several years as a TV scriptwriter on such shows as *The Guiding Light, Tribes,* and *Riviera.* The author of nearly forty novels, Strasser lives with his family in a suburb of New York City.

SWEET DREAMS
Kate Daniel

Jan is terrified to go to sleep. Every night in her dreams she relives the blaze that killed her parents. As her dreams grow more vivid, Jan begins to suspect that the fire wasn't an accident: someone murdered her parents, and she thinks she knows who.

Then Jan starts to walk in her sleep, finding herself mysteriously drawn to a series of midnight fires around town. At first the fires are small, but soon one of Jan's classmates – a girl who accused Jan of starting the fires – is horribly disfigured in the flames that destroy her home.

Is Jan's nightmare coming true? Is she an arsonist – and a killer too?

BABYSITTER'S NIGHTMARE
Kate Daniel

Alice Fleming is trapped in a nightmare. Someone's been breaking into houses all over town, stealing and wrecking furniture. The victims all had one thing in common. Alice babysat their kids. The police are ready to lock Alice up, and even her friends are wondering if Alice has a dark side they never knew.

Then one night Alice cancels a babysitting job, and the substitute sitter is murdered. Alice is desperate to find the real killer. But as she follows the killer's trail, is she walking into a deadly trap set just for her?

SUPER MARIO BROS.
Todd Strasser

Plumbers in a parallel universe!

When an evil reptilian tyrant sets out to merge his world with the human world, it's up to everyone's favourite plumbers to stop him. Mario and Luigi (better known as the Super Mario Bros.) must avoid de-evolution, battle with fireball-shooting goombas, and save Daisy, the beautiful paleontologist-princess – or face the end of the world as they (and we) know it!

Includes eight pages of full-colour stills from the blockbuster film!

TELL MADONNA I'M AT LUNCH
Vici McCarthy

'Madonna on line one!' Yawn. Not her again.

Have you ever wondered how stars got to be stars? Or wanted to gatecrash a celebrity party or simply become very rich and famous? If you haven't, then don't bother to buy this book. But if you have – then rush up to the counter, slap down your dosh and say 'I'll take this and half a pound of sausages, please!'

For this is the book for fans who want fans of their own. By the end of it, and if you have followed all the instructions (almost), you will be so brilliantly famous that when a minor star, like 'Mads', pops round for tea – you can tell her where to go.

ROBIN HOOD PRINCE OF THIEVES
Simon Green

The legend lives on. Like a flaming arrow, Robin of Locksley emerges from the shadows of Sherwood Forest to blaze a path for the poor and downtrodden. With a mighty band of fighting men by his side – Friar Tuck, Will Scarlet, the noble Saracen called Azeem, and others – Robin wages a magnificent war against the vicious Sheriff of Nottingham . . . and an equally passionate campaign for the heart of the beautiful Maid Marian. Wielding his bow and arrow with deadly accuracy, Robin of Locksley transforms himself into a new kind of hero.

THE ADDAMS FAMILY
Elizabeth Faucher

You haven't lived unless you've met the Addams Family! There's Morticia, the loving, caring mother, Gomez, the devoted but manic father, and their children Pugsley and Wednesday. Pugsley collects road signs, and Wednesday's favourite toy is a headless doll. Then, of course, there's Thing, the Addams Family's pet hand, who is always willing to lend one, when two just aren't enough. With the return of Uncle Fester, the long-lost brother of Gomez, after twenty-five years' absence, the family is complete once again. However, he may look like Uncle Fester, he may even sound like him, but can he really be the missing uncle?